Despite being half-awake and confused by her presence, happiness pinged in Myles's chest. "What are you doing here?"

Holland grinned even larger as she spread her hands wide in a grand gesture. "I come bearing housewarming gifts. Mortar for your bricks."

Glancing down, he spotted another large tub, a smaller one, and a plastic shopping bag with several cylinders and tubes.

She walked toward him. "There were so many different kinds to choose from. And without knowing the specifics of the task, the guy at the store made several recommendations. I bought some of each. And this..." She took something out of the bag with the cylinders. "Ta-da!" she sang out as she handed it to him.

It was a trowel. Made for gardening. Not repairing a fireplace.

"Uh, yeah, this is..." She looked so pleased with herself, he didn't have the heart to tell her.

Holland laughed. "I'm just messing with you. That expression on your face was worth it." She reached into the bag again and pulled out the right kind of trowel for the job. "So...I'm ready and I'm here until this afternoon. Put me to work."

She was like a ball of energy bouncing to the car.

He went upstairs to put on a pair of jeans. How many cups of coffee had she drank already? Holland had said she was ready. But was he ready for her?

Dear Reader,

Welcome to Bolan, Maryland, home of Tillbridge Stables and Guesthouse. If you've visited before, welcome back!

Award-winning director and producer Holland Ainsley is in town. The last time she was here was for the filming of her hit movie *Shadow Valley* (in *Her Sweet Temptation*, Tillbridge Stables, Book 2). She's excited to return and visit friends while researching her passion project, a documentary about old houses and vintage architecture. Meeting Myles Alexander has made her trip a lot more interesting. If only the walls of the house he's remodeling could talk.

Myles is searching for peace from past heartbreak. The last thing he's expecting to find is a second chance to open his heart and life to new beginnings with Holland. Starting over and taking chances isn't always easy. But in a town with the slogan Friends and Smiles for Miles Live Here, good things are bound to happen.

I hope you enjoy Holland and Myles's story as well as visiting with the Tillbridge family again. Hearing from readers makes me smile. Instagram, Facebook and my newsletter are three of my favorite places to connect. I look forward to meeting you there. You can find out more about me and my upcoming books at ninacrespo.com.

Wishing you hours of happy reading!

Nina

Second Take at Love

NINA CRESPO

HARLEQUIN

SPECIAL
EDITION

HARLEQUIN®
SPECIAL
EDITION™

Recycling programs
for this product may
not exist in your area.

ISBN-13: 978-1-335-72453-3

Second Take at Love

Copyright © 2023 by Nina Crespo

For questions and comments about the quality of this book,
please contact us at CustomerService@Harlequin.com.

Harlequin Enterprises ULC
22 Adelaide St. West, 41st Floor
Toronto, Ontario M5H 4E3, Canada
www.Harlequin.com

Printed in U.S.A.

Nina Crespo lives in Florida, where she indulges in her favorite passions—the beach, a good glass of wine, date night with her own real-life hero and dancing. Her lifelong addiction to romance began in her teens while on a "borrowing spree" in her older sister's bedroom, where she discovered her first romance novel. Let Nina's sensual contemporary stories feed your own addiction to love, romance and happily-ever-after. Visit her at ninacrespo.com.

Books by Nina Crespo

Harlequin Special Edition

Small Town Secrets

The Chef's Kiss
The Designer's Secret

Tillbridge Stables

The Cowboy's Claim
Her Sweet Temptation
The Cowgirl's Surprise Match

The Fortunes of Texas: Hitting the Jackpot

Fortune's Dream House

The Fortunes of Texas: The Hotel Fortune

An Officer and a Fortune

Visit the Author Profile page
at Harlequin.com for more titles.

Acknowledgments

To my real-life hero and best friend, thank you
for always adding laughter and love to my day.
Megan Broderick, thank you for your encouragement
and always finding a solution. And a big thank-you
to my readers. I hope this addition to the
Small Town Secrets series gives you an enjoyable
escape as you dive into the story and turn the pages.
And as always, my gratitude to Life, Breath
and Inspiration for leading the way.

Chapter One

Holland Ainsley stood in her bedroom, holding up a vintage logoed T-shirt in each hand. She barely had room in her suitcase for one of them, but the orange shirt emblemized with Summer Party intertwined with surf boards and palm trees, and the beige one with a peace symbol, were two of her favorites.

She tucked the orange one into her bag on the queen-size bed and set the beige one aside. Packing light had been her intention, but…

Her phone rang on the nightstand. Recognizing the ringtone, she answered it. "Good morning, sunshine."

During the beat of silence, it was easy for her to imagine Burke Layton's semi amused expression. He wasn't the sunny, radiant type. Right then, his dark brows were probably raised slightly above the bold, black-framed glasses that accentuated the hint of arrogance in his blue eyes.

"When are you leaving for the airport?" he asked.

Giving in to the impulse, she grabbed the beige T-shirt and stuffed it in her bag as well. "A car is picking me up in thirty minutes. Why?"

"Cancel it. I'll be there in ten."

It was just like Burke to skip past hello and head straight to a plan. But planning was *her* job. His was financier. That was the agreement the two of them had made when they'd formed a film production company together. Six months into their venture with A & L Productions, he still seemed to grapple with his role of *silent* partner.

Sitting on her suitcase, she forced the top and bottom closer together and tugged the zipper shut. "You *do* know there's a difference between offering me a ride and ordering me to go with you?"

"Ordering you?" Burke chuckled. "Trust me, I'm well aware that I can't order you to do anything. But we need to meet before you go."

The seriousness in his tone made Holland pause before sliding her suitcase to the floor. As she straightened the hem of her white boho blouse over the waistband of her faded jeans, warmth from exertion flushed in her light brown cheeks.

What was going on? And why was he being so mysterious? She almost asked, but the fact that he hadn't told her right from the start meant they probably needed to discuss it face-to-face.

"I need fifteen minutes, not ten," she said.

"See you then."

After canceling the ride her assistant had arranged for her to Los Angeles International Airport, Holland went through a mental checklist for her trip to Maryland. Her comfy lace-up combat boots were already in her suitcase. She'd also thrown in a light jacket and a couple of sweaters. Spring on the East Coast was always iffy as far as the weather was concerned. She'd also brought a nice dress and shoes to go with everything. And her other must-haves were packed, too.

The green backpack with her wallet, passport, laptop and trusty Nikon camera was on the dresser. Between the Nikon and the camera on her phone, she'd come back with plenty of photos as ideas for her passion project, a potential documentary about old houses.

As far as her passport, Holland always took it with her now when she traveled. With productions currently happening in multiple locations, she never knew when someone might need her to come to the set. Usually issues could be handled with a phone or a video chat, but sometimes an in-person visit was best.

For instance, just last week there had been a camera equipment problem in Canada. Laurel, the holiday rom-com's director, was fairly new to the position. She'd handled the problem, but during their phone call, Holland had picked up on the high level of stress in the woman's voice. And she'd understood where it came from—a feeling of being responsible for everything but also that nothing was in your control. For a woman in a male-dominated field, the desire to get it right and prove yourself made the weight even heavier.

Holland had flown down to Canada that past weekend. Working together, she and Laurel had adjusted the production schedule to get things back on track and bring the filming of the movie in close to budget.

Satisfied she had everything she needed, Holland secured the pack on top of her suitcase. After resting a pair of aviator sunglasses in front of her dark auburn afro ponytail, she took her things downstairs.

The stiletto heels of her ankle boots tapped on the tile floor as she rolled her bags past her sunlit living room decorated in hues of purple and beige. The space was just as tidy as the expansive dining room on the left with a table for eight she hardly ever used.

She'd given up on keeping plants alive shortly after moving into the four-bedroom house three years ago. Between travel and her hectic work schedule, they didn't stand a chance. Instead, table- and floor-size abstract sculptures in square nooks in the walls and in the corners added focal points in every room.

As she reached the front door, her phone chimed with a notification that someone was at the entrance to the driveway. A black Range Rover waited at the security gate. *Burke.* Tapping in a code, she gave the vehicle access to the property.

Outside, the luxury SUV rounded the circular

drive bordering the lawn and parked in front of the house.

A dark-haired driver got out to take her suitcase and open the back passenger-side door.

Returning the driver's friendly good morning with a smile and a thank-you, Holland got inside.

Burke sat in the back behind the driver.

As she fastened her seat belt, she gave her business partner a saccharine-sweet smile. "Good morning. Again. Or do you prefer *buenos días* or *bonjour*? I want to know how to greet you when I ambush *you* with a meeting right before your vacation."

Burke raked a hand through his short black hair. "Good luck with that. I don't take vacations."

He wasn't lying. His attitude, along with his white pullover, jeans and tennis shoes, may have appeared laid-back, but to the discerning eye they whispered "expensive". His high-end clothing also mirrored the rewards he'd reaped for working constantly.

Two years older than her at age thirty, he'd made his first million by his midtwenties in the tech industry.

With his height and build, he could have easily walked a fashion runway like she had before she'd left the modeling industry seven years ago to pursue a career in film. But he'd tried acting before making his bankroll.

His family was an old-guard Hollywood dynasty of award-winning performers. However, Burke's budding acting career had come to a swift halt after he'd starred in three bad movies. Not a terrible thing, since it led him to form his first company.

A mutual friend had introduced Holland and Burke at a house party, insisting they needed to be on each other's contact list. That chance meeting had led to their friends-only relationship, and it had also paid off.

After Holland's recent split with her old business partners—they'd wanted to keep making sequels and spin-offs of her directorial hit, *Shadow Valley*, and she didn't—Burke had approached her about going into business with him.

He'd ventured back into movies by funding independent films but now wanted a hand in developing projects.

She'd walked away from the old partnership with no further obligations to them, but the trade-off was the loss of funding to bring to fruition the options and scripts she'd acquired as part of the split. Partnering with Burke had solved her financial problem. And they shared the same vision of developing a range of narratives, from fanciful to inspiring, that were grounded in solid storytelling.

Burke glanced at her suitcase in the back of the SUV. "Are you planning to come back or are you running away?"

"That depends on what you tell me."

As the chauffeur drove toward the front gate that opened automatically, Burke handed her a manila envelope. "This was delivered to me yesterday."

Unease moved through Holland as she opened it and slid out a photo.

It showed two people standing on a balcony in a passionate embrace.

She recognized the location. It was the guest lodge on the property of the closed ski resort where they were filming in Canada.

The face of one of the people in the photo was obscured by the hood of their jacket. But the blond-haired guy they were with was clearly visible. It was her ex-boyfriend Nash Moreland. "Okay, I still don't understand why you're showing me this."

"The person he's with is Gina Landry."

Gina? His very engaged costar? "Oh no…"

"*Oh shit* is more like it. If this were to get out, it would be disastrous for her career."

Gina was a former child star. The roles the brunette played skewed toward the girl next door. In the movie she and Nash were currently shooting, she was cast as an accident-prone, endearing angel trying to earn her silver wings by helping Nash's character, a grumpy cattle rancher, find love.

Reinforcing her wholesome image, she'd just become engaged to a guy back in her hometown in Nebraska. The reality series spotlighting the couple's wedding preparations was set to premiere just before the movie's release.

Yet Gina had put her career at risk, not to mention the film, by having a fling with Nash?

Holland and Nash had dated after she'd directed him in *Shadow Valley*. Natural attraction, and the

ease of just being together, because they understood
the expectations of each other's careers, had led them
into a relationship.

But after two years of being together, Holland had
grown tired of mostly engaging with Nash's carefully
cultivated actor persona. She'd wanted to connect
with the real Nash, not the guy who did everything
for show. After a long heart-to-heart conversation,
he'd vowed to change, but he couldn't let go of the
façade. It had been hard to accept he wouldn't. Not
even for her. She'd broken up with him.

Her ex did have charming down to a science, and
the whole *action star with a bad-boy vibe* going for
him. Maybe that had been the attraction for Gina.

Still, the actors should have known better than to
get involved. Tell-all shows, magazines and blogs always had people waiting to catch wind of a scandal-
ous on-set affair between costars.

Holland peered at the photo. "Are you one hundred percent sure this is Gina? We can't see her
face…"

"It's her. She and Nash confirmed they were together. They claim it was just that one night. They
thought they'd been discreet."

"Well, somebody noticed them," she pointed out.
"Who was it? A freelancer or a tabloid photographer?"

"Neither. It was snapped by one of the security
guards. He tried to cover up his involvement by having his girlfriend deliver the photo, along with a letter threatening to sell it unless we paid them. Once

we traced everything to the guard, we reminded him
about the repercussions of breaching the NDA he'd
signed." Burke glanced over her and his lips quirked
with a small sardonic smile. "After that, he was ex-
tremely cooperative about giving us access to his
phone and computers. All the photos we found were
like this one. Fortunately, he never got a clear shot of
Gina. We wiped everything we found with her and
Nash from the security guard's and the girlfriend's
devices."

"Great. So it's taken care of."

"Possibly. But Gina's people are also concerned
about rumors that were already circulating about
Nash and Gina on set. They want them buried or to
be able to cast doubt on their validity."

Holland narrowed her eyes. "How will they do
that?"

"The easiest way is to plant a rumor that he's with
someone other than Gina."

"Who?"

Burke's gaze settled on her face.

"*Me?* No way!"

He stalled the rest of her forthcoming objection
with a raised hand. "I have to agree. They're right
about this. You and Nash have a history, and you
were there at the time this picture was taken. It's
plausible the person Nash is seeing is you."

"But it isn't. We broke up over a year ago, and
there's no way I would ever get back with him—
even for one night."

Ending her relationship with Nash had been hard.

Coming to terms with the fact that she'd been more invested in the relationship than him had been even harder.

As difficult as facing that heartbreak had been, it *had* clarified where her focus needed to be. On her career. Since then, she'd poured her time and energy into her work.

Burke continued his campaign to win her over. "It would just be a rumor. People's imaginations would do the rest. Especially since he just broke up with his last girlfriend. The story could be as simple as he needed comfort, and you hooked up with him for the hell of it. Neither you nor Nash would need to make a comment about it."

A laugh of disbelief slipped out of Holland. "So you want to replace the truth about him and Gina with a salacious rumor about me being Nash's one-night rebound?"

"It's a lot better than what *could* happen if we don't get ahead of this." Frustration shadowed Burke's grim expression. "Our movie is riding on Gina's key audience, and they won't go for her cheating on her fiancé. This movie could end up doomed before they even finish filming it. And trying to rehab her image over this mistake would take time and money we don't have. The film's budget is already tight, mainly because of Nash's and Gina's salaries, and it's gotten even tighter because of the delay that probably could have been avoided."

Holland huffed out a breath. The camera equipment issue had happened because of a miscommunication. It wasn't an ideal occurrence, but anyone who'd been in the position of supervising multiple people had been through the experience...even Burke. Choosing Laurel as the director and handling the casting of the film were Holland's choices. Was he doubting her decisions or trying to blame her in some way for their current problems?

As she considered those possibilities, her own frustration mounted. "I understand that we have an image crisis on our hands, but in Canada, I watched the dailies and viewed the raw footage from prior days of filming. Under Laurel's direction, Gina and Nash are brilliant. Even with the cost of the delay, which Laurel has already cut down by adjusting the filming schedule, every dollar we're spending on this project is worth it."

She and Burke locked gazes for a few long seconds. This was their first disagreement as partners. How they worked through this problem would set the tone for the future.

He released a long breath. "Arguing about this won't solve anything. The truth is, it won't matter how brilliant the film is if a scandal takes us down. As partners, we need to be in sync. The ball's in your court on this one. What do you want to do?"

Chapter Two

Holland stood with the rest of the passengers from her flight at the baggage carousel. After almost nine hours of travel, she was glad to finally be in Baltimore. Now she just had a two-hour drive to Tillbridge Horse Stable and Guesthouse near the town of Bolan, Maryland.

Close to three years had passed since she'd last been on the property directing *Shadow Valley*. Back then, the production of the movie had consumed much of her time. But when she had taken a moment to look up, the gorgeous view of sloping pastures and horses grazing in the distance had been like a mini vacation.

Over the last couple months, the anticipation she'd usually felt for the next big film project had started to wane. It had gotten so bad, she couldn't concentrate. And when her mind would drift, often it would settle on her memories of Tillbridge.

A couple of weeks ago, when actress Chloe Daniels had called, and it felt like a sign.

Chloe had starred in *Shadow Valley*, and they had become friends. The actress was also married to one of the owners of the stable and guesthouse.

During their call, Holland had mentioned thinking about the property, and Chloe had suggested she make time for a visit. Feeling drained and at a loss for how to get her spark back, Holland had immediately started clearing her schedule so she could take a vacation.

That act alone, plus realizing Bolan was the perfect place to research her passion project, had given her a bit of a boost. For the next two weeks, maybe three, she would combine a little fun research with pleasure, and she couldn't wait.

An alarm sounded from the baggage carousel. Luggage slid from a chute onto the spinning belt.

Someone nudged her arm. "Excuse me," a woman said. "Can I offer you a ride?"

Holland's firm refusal quickly morphed into happiness as she registered Chloe's voice.

But Chloe's appearance made Holland do a double take. Her friend's eyes were swallowed by a pair of wide-frame glasses. A long black wig also covered most of her pretty brown face. Maybe she was trying on a look for an upcoming role?

Smiling, they shared a sisterly hug.

"What are you doing here?" Holland asked. "I thought I was meeting you at Tillbridge in the morning?"

"I wanted to give you my car tonight so you wouldn't have to rent one. Hand me your backpack. I'll hold it while you wade in and get your luggage."

Holland retrieved her suitcase, and on the way out of the terminal, she canceled her rental car reservation.

Twenty minutes later, they got into Chloe's blue four-door in the airport parking lot.

As Chloe settled behind the wheel, she stripped off the wig and glasses. Shaking out her own dark curls, she released a breath of relief. "I'm so glad I can finally take this disguise off."

"Is that what the wig and glasses were about? I thought you were breaking in the look for a part."

"No, thank goodness! I didn't schedule personal security, and Tristan couldn't come with me. The only way I could get him out of protective husband mode was to promise I would wear a disguise in the airport."

Holland fastened her seat belt. "You didn't have to do this. I really didn't mind renting my own transportation."

"I know." Chloe secured her own seat belt and started the car. "But I couldn't wait to see you. I'm also planning to pamper you as much as possible to remind you that you're on vacation. You have a car to use and a nice suite at the guesthouse since you're refusing to stay at my place. And you'll be treated to some great meals."

"Stop trying to make me feel guilty about not staying at your house. It's not that I didn't want to, but you just got home after weeks of being away filming your next movie. You and Tristan need to enjoy your time together, not look after a houseguest. And I'm not sponging off you for meals, either."

"Oh, that's too bad." Chloe feigned a sad look as she pulled out of the parking space. "Dominic was really looking forward to cooking for you, but I'll tell him the plan has changed."

"Whoa! Not so fast. Dominic as in *Dominic Crawford*?"

"Yep."

Dominic Crawford, television personality and founder of Frost & Flame restaurant, was her favorite chef on the planet. Eating his version of brownbutter lime shrimp with Carolina Gold rice grits was like consuming a bite of heaven. She ordered it whenever she visited his LA restaurant. Or at least she used to order it.

Chloe gave her a quick glance as she drove to the exit. "What's that look about? I thought you'd be happy about Dominic cooking for you."

"I am. It's not Dominic. I was thinking about how much I missed eating at Frost & Flame. I made the mistake of introducing Nash to the restaurant, and now it seems like every time I'm there, he is, too. And he always makes a big show of stopping by my table."

"That definitely sounds like Nash. So I guess the story I heard from the makeup artist on set before I left isn't true—you and Nash aren't rekindling your relationship."

So the whisper campaign had already started. That's how the false story was circulating. Resignation dropped like a rock inside Holland. Judgments would be made about her and Nash's "reunion." But on the flight, she'd made peace with her decision. The cast and crew, along with Laurel, were giving their all to get the movie finished. No one needed Nash and Gina's mistake hanging over the set, tarnishing everyone's hard work. Not to mention the added stress for Laurel. Enduring a rumor that she didn't even have to acknowledge was a small sacrifice for Holland to make.

But Chloe was her friend. Holland wasn't going to lie to her. "In a way, Nash and I are together…"

As Chloe merged with nighttime traffic on the interstate, Holland explained the Nash and Gina situation.

"So you're making a sacrifice for the team and Nash." Chloe gave a subtle eye roll. "It makes sense, but I hate that you have to get involved. Breaking up with him took an emotional toll on you."

"But I've moved on." Long seconds later, Chloe still hadn't agreed. Holland added. "I'm not still grieving over him if that's what you're thinking."

Chloe sighed. "What I'm thinking is that he shouldn't have put you in this position in the first place. On-set affairs are always so messy, on the other hand, I'm not surprised Nash indulged in one, but Gina? She's practically on every rom-com casting director's wish list. Why would she put her career at risk? And then her engagement. Does her fiancé know?"

"I doubt it. A brokenhearted fiancé is probably too much for her people to handle right now, so they'll avoid it. Or maybe Gina's hoping he'll never find out."

"Hiding an affair from your fiancé to protect your image. I think that's even worse than him finding out. I could never hurt Tristan that way."

"You wouldn't, because you value your marriage over your career."

"It's not just me. Tristan feels the same way about his responsibilities at Tillbridge. But my agent says someday that choice could stall my career."

"Do you worry that you might regret making that decision?"

Chloe offered up a delicate shrug. "Would I feel disappointed about losing a part or an opportunity I really wanted? Yes. Would I regret making the decision? No. As much as I love acting, I love Tristan more. Not to mention, Hollywood is fickle. Too many wrinkles. Ten additional pounds, or consecutive movies that flop, and my star power goes down the drain. But I know I can always count on Tristan. He's a good man and he loves me. What we have is forever."

Holland took in what Chloe said. What she described with Tristan sounded wonderful. When things were good with Nash, she'd actually allowed herself to fantasize about what forever might look like for them. Dedication to her job and people depending on her had been the main hurdles in the vision. She'd struggled to see herself giving up what she was passionate about—the career she'd worked so hard to build—for a relationship. She just couldn't.

"Well," Chloe added, "the good thing is, while you're here, you can forget about the Gina and Nash situation and just focus on *you*. Last time we talked, you said the research part of this trip involves historic houses. Are you interested in ones with an architectural significance or ones that are tied to a historical event?"

"I won't rule them out, but I'm more interested in the backstories of the people who lived in them. There are so many unique stories about homes and the people connected to them that aren't considered historical, but they're still compelling."

"That's…interesting."

From Chloe's polite comment, she found the topic far from riveting. At least her eyes hadn't glazed over like Burke's had when he'd first heard the idea. But uncovering details that would catch someone's interest was part of a documentarian's job.

And Holland was up for the challenge. "It will be interesting. But first, I have to find the houses."

Chloe tapped her finger on the steering wheel. "Now that I think about it, I may know of a place. I'm not sure where I heard about it, but if I'm remembering the story correctly, one of the locals was afraid to travel outside Bolan. He fell in love with a painter who came to town. They moved in together. To show him the world, she used the walls of their home like a canvas and painted the places she'd visited."

Holland's interest piqued. "Wow. That's exactly the type of thing I'm looking for! How long ago was this? Are the murals still intact?"

"This happened a few decades ago, I think. But the murals aren't the best part of the story."

"What happened?" Impatience teased at Holland as Chloe's attention shifted to changing lanes and accelerating past a slow-moving car.

"Her paintings encouraged the man to get past his fear. They left Bolan together."

Excitement made Holland turn toward her friend. "Please tell me you know where this house is located and that you know the owners."

"I don't, but Tristan probably does." Chloe glanced at her and chuckled. "You look like a child who just got an early birthday gift. Most people would call research work, but you really do consider this project the perfect vacation."

"I do." As Holland sat back in the seat, she didn't hold back a smile. Nothing, including Nash and Gina's Hollywood scandal, was going to ruin her vacation.

The next morning, Holland exited the glass double doors of the guesthouse carrying her backpack.

Green rocking chairs swayed on the porch of the two-story white building with green trim. The air was filled with earthy scents of rich dirt, freshly cut grass and, of course, horses.

As she walked down the steps toward the front parking lot, the floral midi skirt that was as blue as the sky that she'd paired with her peace sign T-shirt and her favorite brown boots slightly rose and clung to her legs.

Unable to resist, she paused taking in the view of horses grazing in one of the surrounding white, fenced-in fields. A sense of peacefulness settled over her.

On the way out, the clerk at the desk in the lobby had wished her a good morning. How could she not have a wonderful day in a place this beautiful?

A short time later, she was in her borrowed blue care. As she sped past modern two-story houses separated by acres of land, the map app on her phone gave her directions to the Oakview Road address Chloe had given her for the house with the murals.

She might have time to visit three homes today, the one Chloe had mentioned and two others she'd discovered on the internet. One of them supposedly had an interesting wine cellar. The other, some kind of maze in the backyard. But she was starting with the mural house. The story her friend had told her about the painter and recluse was so intriguing.

Miles later, older-looking clapboard homes sat back in the trees. A few of them had barns with horses or cows grazing in a nearby field.

The people in those places might have homes

with interesting backstories. Or they might be able to point her in the direction of people who did.

Chloe had once told her that in Bolan, everyone knew everybody's business. That quality, which some might find bothersome, signaled a possible gold mine to her in finding leads.

As she continued her drive, the landscape changed to mostly fields.

"In eight hundred feet, turn right on to Oakview Road," the voice on the map app said.

At the unmarked intersection, Holland complied.

"You have arrived at your destination."

What? This couldn't be it. All she saw was wide-open grassy fields and clusters of trees…but no houses. Not even a barn or shed. Maybe the house was farther up?

Holland kept driving. As she reached a grouping of oaks and sycamores on the right-hand side, she caught a glimpse of a tall structure.

She made the turn down a gravel road, and as she rounded a curve, a three-story house came into view.

It had seen better days.

The white siding was worn and faded, and tiles were absent from the dark gray pitched roof. Spindles from the railing on the wraparound porch were also missing. Some of the gray shutters hung askew on the sides of the windows. Only one of the windows wasn't boarded up, but the glass in the windowpane was broken.

But even in its sorry state, it had character and a presence. The people who had once lived there had probably sat on the porch conversing with family and friends or while keeping an eye on their children playing outside.

The multiple windows on the first and second floors would have let in warmth and natural light during the day. And the window below the inverted V of the roof most likely provided the best view of the landscape and sunrises and sunsets hovering over the tops of the trees.

Based on what Chloe had said, she'd assumed someone still lived there. This place looked as if it were possibly abandoned. Still, that didn't diminish the story about the local man and the artist who'd once lived there or the murals. Hopefully some of the woman's paintings were still intact.

Holland parked, took her camera from her backpack on the seat and got out.

Approaching the house, she snapped a few photos.

Aside from the camera clicks, the only sounds were chirping birds, rustling trees and the soles of her boots crunching on the gravel driveway that turned into grass a few yards from the house.

Shouldn't the foliage have been more overgrown? Maybe someone was keeping an eye on the place after all.

Avoiding broken bricks on the stairs, she walked up to the porch.

The front door was partially open.

Curiosity over whether a mural was just behind the door got the best of her.

As she started to nudge the door, the hinges

creaked. Aided by the wind, it opened farther, as if welcoming her inside.

Goose bumps rose on her arms, but the excitement of a possible discovery overrode unease. She stepped across the threshold, and the planks in the dull-looking wood floor groaned beneath her feet.

Light from a window that wasn't boarded up and the rear French double doors illuminated the bottom floor. Wallpaper with a faded design of tiny red flowers was peeling from the walls.

A slab of plywood sat propped on the wall near the window that wasn't boarded up. Someone had taken the wood off from outside the window and brought it in.

Holland called out, "Hello…is anybody here?" Sliding her sunglasses to the top of her head, she glanced up the staircase on the left.

Her voice echoed, hovering like the musty smell of neglect and particles of dust floating in the air.

She walked toward the back of the house, passing the large brick fireplace on the right. The kitchen farther back to the left of the French doors was stripped of appliances. The space across from it that had once been the formal dining room had a dark wood starburst design inlaid in the floor and a ceiling border with a floral motif.

Had the past owners preferred to enjoy a meal in the formal dining room or in front of the fireplace? If she'd lived there, she would have chosen the fireplace. The slow, flickering flames and the pops and crackles from the wood would have been so relaxing after a long day.

Holland hung the camera around her neck by its thick strap. She ambled to the fireplace and ran her fingers over the dust-coated mantel situated between two thick columns of brick. It wasn't ready for logs to be lit in the firebox, but with a little TLC, it could easily become the grand centerpiece it once was.

One of the front bricks on the mantel shifted toward her. Behind it, there was a small gap between two bricks on the column. Something was poking out of it.

She stuck her hand in the space behind the front brick, but she couldn't quite reach the gap. Wiggling it around, she tried to slide it forward a bit more. Suddenly, to her dismay, bricks on the mantel and the attached column collapsed like falling dominoes crashing at her feet.

"What are you doing in my house?" a man's angry voice boomed.

As Holland spun toward the source, her heart leaped into her throat, transforming her scream into a surprised squeak.

A big, tall man with sepia-brown skin and neatly trimmed black hair stared at her so intently as he stood in one of the open French doors, she couldn't pull her gaze from his. Not to mention, he had a face she didn't want to look away from. His thick, evenly shaped brows drew attention to his gaze. Even in the dim light, she could tell his eyes weren't just an ordinary brown hue.

They guy who looked to be in his early thirties strode inside, and his long-sleeved burgundy shirt stretched over his chest, highlighting the play of well-toned muscle underneath. The dark beige cargo pants and boots he had on were made for the outdoors.

But what was she doing checking the guy out? She should have been at the front door by now, running toward the car. And it was way too late to pick up a brick to defend herself. All she had left was her precious camera.

As he came closer, she held it up along with her other hand. "I was just looking around."

"No, you were destroying my property." He stopped a few feet away. "What's your name? Forget it." Clearly annoyed, he waved away his own question and pointed to the front door. "Leave and don't come back. And tell your friends to stay away, too. If I catch any of you vandalizing my property again, I'll call the police. And no matter how much your parents beg me not to, I'm pressing charges."

Parents? How old did he think she was? "But—"

He pointed to the front door. "Go before I change my mind."

From the look in his gorgeous, coppery-brown eyes, he wasn't interested in hearing an explanation. And she *was* trespassing. If he found out she was a full-grown adult instead of a teen like he thought, he might just make good on his threat to call the cops. She'd find a way to contact him later and offer to pay for the damages.

"Okay...sorry." She hurried out the front door.

A part of her actually felt like she was a teenager again and had gotten busted by one of her teachers for doing something she shouldn't…and had been let off the hook. Good thing none of her teachers had looked like this tall, dark-haired stranger when she was in high school. Otherwise, she would have gotten in trouble a lot more often.

As she drove off, the guy stood on his porch with his arms crossed over his chest, just staring at her.

Chapter Three

Myles Alexander inspected the damage to the fireplace and the pile of bricks on the floor. None of the fallen bricks were usable. He'd have to buy new ones to repair the mantel and the column.

Damn kids. Didn't they have anything better to do than destroy property?

A few weeks ago, Tristan Tillbridge, a local man who owned a horse stable in the area, had been driving by the house when he noticed smoke coming from the backyard. He'd chased a group of teenagers from the house, and thankfully managed to get the small blaze they'd started under control.

A vision of the girl Myles had just chased off flickered in his mind. When Tristan had mentioned vandals during their phone conservation after the incident, he'd imagined the hardened type who just didn't care what they did.

She'd looked at him as if she'd been caught with her hand in the cookie jar. And maybe like she'd wanted to apologize to him.

Had he been too hard on her? He could have just given her a stern lecture about making better choices.

Not that it mattered now. She was gone. And he had a fireplace that would now be added to a long list of repairs.

Releasing a sigh, Myles massaged the back of his neck. This situation was partially his fault. He knew better than to let the house just sit without proper care. But after losing Sydney…

As Myles stood, sadness weighed down a heavy breath. He hadn't even known his wife had bought a property in Maryland. She'd purchased it before she'd passed away unexpectedly, two and a half years ago.

During their six-year marriage, Sydney used to joke about leaving their life in Philadelphia to re-model a quiet place in the country. She would talk about them transforming it together. Well, mainly he would do the transforming.

Amusement shaded his rising memories. She'd been a danger to herself or anything in the vicinity with any type of repair tool in her hands. Yet, ironi-cally, he'd met her eight years ago at a home improve-ment store. Sydney had flagged him down and asked for his opinion on a paint color for her kitchen. At the time he'd been twenty-four and working in construction. She'd just started her first job out of college, working for a health-store chain.

There had been an instant spark between them, and they'd fallen head over heels in love. A year later, they'd gotten married. Over the course of their marriage, they'd gotten new jobs and promotions. A home in the suburbs. And not enough downtime for vacations or to just be together.

Bittersweet regret expanded inside of Myles. If he'd done things differently, maybe they wouldn't have gone through so many difficulties in their relationship.

Putting all "what ifs" from his marriage back into the mental space he'd reserved for them, Myles grabbed a flashlight from his toolbox.

According to the last inspection, the foundation and frame were both solid. A previous owner had replaced all the lead pipes with updated materials. Aside from cosmetic wear and tear, the other main issues were the electrical system and the roof.

Upstairs was in better shape than the first floor, and so was the third-floor loft. And the smaller bathroom on the second floor was operational. Otherwise, he would have had to spend money on a hotel room.

Once he aired out the house and cleaned up the room where he planned to sleep, he'd rough it with the inflatable mattress he'd packed in the back of his SUV.

Hopefully he'd only be there a week, two at the most. He was finalizing meeting dates today with potential contractors to get estimates on repairs. The other task he needed to manage was finding a caretaker who could keep a closer eye on things after he'd left.

Myles's phone vibrated with a familiar chime. He answered it. "Hello."

"Hey," his brother, Dante, responded. "How's the drive? Are you hitting much traffic?"

"I'm already here." Myles left the loft and headed downstairs. "I took off earlier than expected. The builder I was supposed to meet with in New Jersey canceled."

"Was it the meeting with Odom Construction, the one I suggested you bump in the first place?"

Working for Dante's tech company in New York, specializing in construction management software, had its pros and cons. Pros—he liked his brother, and he enjoyed being the company's operations manager. Cons—Dante knew too much about his schedule and was always making suggestions about how he should manage his time, especially when it came to taking time off.

Ignoring Dante's question, Myles continued to the first floor. "They rescheduled. We're meeting in a couple of weeks."

"A couple of *weeks*? Won't it take longer than that for you to remodel the house?"

"I haven't made up my mind about remodeling it." At the bottom of the landing, Myles turned off the flashlight and walked out the front door. "I'll know what I'm doing after I meet with the contractors and find a good caretaker to oversee things."

"Honestly, I think you need to rethink that plan for several reasons."

"And if you say that one of them is the *C* word, I'm hanging up on you."

Closure. Myles had heard it so many times, he'd banned it from his vocabulary. Hours of talk therapy had already gotten him to the place he needed to be when it came to losing Sydney.

"I wasn't going to use the *C* word," Dante replied. "You said you found it, and I believe you. But you'll never be able to just sit back and let someone else manage the remodel. Having your attention split between here and there won't help either of us get anything done. Stay there and oversee the work. Better yet, do it yourself. It's been a while since you got your hands dirty."

"Oh so epoxying the floor in your garage and repairing your bathroom sink doesn't count as getting my hands dirty?"

"That's amateur stuff. Or maybe your skills have gotten so rusty that's all you can handle now."

"Somebody's got jokes today. Don't quit your day job. Being a comedian is not your thing."

Dante chuckled. "No need to get sensitive. But seriously, back in the day, when you flipped houses, you enjoyed it."

And it had helped pay the bills. At the age of eighteen, after losing their mom, he'd become Dante's legal guardian. For three years, he'd been responsible for his younger brother until Dante had reached legal age. It hadn't been easy for either of them, but luckily, his baby brother had been a brainiac, more interested in books than causing trouble.

But Dante was also right about him enjoying it. Working on houses, outside of his construction job, hadn't felt like a chore. And some days, methodical tasks like painting a wall or laying a floor had been his own form of meditation. Finding a diamond in the rough and turning it into something special took hard work but also had incredible rewards.

It could be nice to experience that feeling again.

Myles walked down the porch steps and glanced back at the house. "I don't know. I'm still trying to figure out why I'm here and what she was thinking. It's weird."

"Because the place reminds you of Sydney?"

Confusion laced with sadness moved through Myles. "No, it's just the opposite. I don't see her in this house at all. She needed to be around people. This place would have been too remote for her. And sure, I like older homes, but this isn't what I would have chosen. It's too run down. She would have known that."

Or at least Sydney should have.

As if he'd been reading his mind, Dante interjected. "But she also knew that you're good at fixing things. Doing the remodel might give you that answer to why she bought it. Or maybe you won't find the answer and just end up with a good investment. Either way, you're overthinking things, as usual."

Maybe he was overthinking the situation. He had the money to put into the house. And the chance to do hands on work again with a remodel was tempting.

Myles mulled it over in his mind. "You could be right."

"I usually am."

Dante was usually right *some* of the time. Myles huffed a chuckle to himself. A second call buzzing in on his phone halted Myles's forthcoming response.

It was Tristan Tillbridge. He really needed to talk to him. "I've got another call coming in. I have to go. I'll keep you posted on my status."

Holland strolled into Pasture Lane restaurant located in the twenty-room guesthouse.

She'd traded in her brick dust–covered boots for a pair of high-heeled red ones. She'd also changed into a pair of jeans that made her feel good whenever she wore them and a cream sweater that fit like a gentle hug.

Inside the wood-floored foyer of the restaurant, a college-aged guy wearing a navy button-down and black slacks stood behind the host podium. "Hello. Do you have a reservation with us tonight?"

"I'm dining with the Tillbridges. Can you point out their table?"

"I'd be happy to. They're over there."

"Thank you." Holland veered left.

Pale wood floors gave the space an open feel, and tall potted plants brought inviting warmth.

On the opposite side of the room, a wall of glass

overlooked a lighted wood deck. Holland recognized the courtyard with trees beyond it as the one visible from the sliding door in her second-floor suite.

As she approached the long table, Rina Tillbridge and her fiancé, Scott Halsey, spotted her first.

Rina owned the local café, Brewed Haven. She'd provided desserts for the cast and crew of *Shadow Valley* during the filming of the movie. Scott had been Nash's stunt double in the film.

"Holland!" Rina's brown face lit up with a lovely smile. The skirt of her blue dress and her long, dark braids flowed around her as she hurried over to Holland and rocked her in a long, tight hug.

Scott finally got his turn. The muscular blond grinned. "It's good to see you again."

"You, too."

Zurie and Mace each gave her a hug.

No one would doubt Zurie and Rina were sisters. Similarities shown in their features. But tonight, there was one noticeable difference other than Zurie's black hair pulled back in a sleek ponytail—she had a distinct new-bride glow. And when the naturally tanned sheriff deputy glanced to Zurie, all he felt for her was clearly evident in his gaze.

Holland didn't mean to keep staring at the couple. But she envied their closeness. She'd never really experienced that with anyone. A sudden sense of wistfulness drove her to look away.

As Zurie took a seat at the end of the table, Mace sat to her left and Holland beside him. Rina and Scott also took their seats. Three chairs sat empty on the other end.

A dark-haired server topped off water glasses and took Holland's wine order.

"I've been looking forward to this meal all day," Mace said.

"Me, too." Zurie glanced around the dining area. "From the number of reservations, word got out that Dominic and Philippa are in the kitchen tonight."

The married chef duo were a powerhouse on the cooking scene. Philippa Gayle Crawford was also head chef of Pasture Lane restaurant and often made guest appearances on her husband's show, *Farm to Fork with Dominic Crawford*.

Rina gave a small clap of excitement. "Whenever Dominic and Philippa cook together, the food is extra amazing."

Scott paused in taking a sip of beer from his glass. "Does anyone have an ETA on Chloe and Tristan?"

Holland waited a beat before chiming in. "I got a text from Chloe on my way here. She said they were about fifteen minutes out."

Chloe had also apologized for sending her to the wrong house for the murals. Apparently, Tristan had misunderstood what she'd asked him.

Scott pointed to the open seats. "Aside from Tristan and Chloe, who else is joining us?"

Rina replied. "Maybe Layla or Bastian?"

"It would have to be Layla," Mace said. "Bastian is out of town."

Rina looked to Holland. "You'll like Layla. She

co-owns the dress shop in town with Bastian's grandmother. Definitely stop by there if shopping is on your
agenda. Layla is a designer, and some of her originals
are sold in the shop."

"I'll definitely do that." Holland thanked the server
delivering her chardonnay and baskets of warm bread
for the table.

The sweet, warm, yeasty smell wafted in the air.

Zurie took a roll from one of the baskets and then
offered the basket to Mace. "So, Holland, it's not
just work? Fun is also part of the plan in the midst
of scouting locations for your new movie?"

Holland accepted the basket from Mace. As she
snagged a roll, her thoughts went back to how lonely
and empty she'd felt before Chloe had convinced her
to come to Maryland. And how much she'd needed
a change. But this wasn't the time or place to bare
her soul.

"I'm not exactly scouting locations," Holland replied. "It's more like research to see if I can develop
an idea about a documentary featuring houses…"

She explained the premise to the group, then told
them about the houses that had been on her list that
afternoon. Time got away from her and she hadn't
made it to the maze house. And the owners of the
wine cellar house were still on vacation. They'd forgotten to tell her but had been so sweet and apologetic when she'd contacted them. And then there was
the dead-end search for the mural house.

Remembering Mace was a deputy sheriff, she
skipped the part about trespassing and running into

the not-so-friendly homeowner. But he wasn't easy to forget. Especially the intensity of his gaze and how his gorgeous eyes might change with a laugh, a smile or subtle sexy smirk. Something she'd never find out.

Rina shook her head. "A place with murals where a recluse used to live with a painter?" "I've never heard of it. It sounds like one of those stories that gets passed around."

"I'm going with myth." Mace lowered his voice. "'Cause if it were true, the mayor would be advertising it as a must-see attraction. Hell, he'd draw stick figure murals himself if he thought it would bring in tourists."

"Stop!" Zurie playfully whacked his arm. "He's not that bad."

"Shh." Rina suppressed a laugh. "Mayor Ashford and his wife just came in."

Gerard Ashford and his wife, Poppy, waved at various people around the room. The middle-aged couple were the perfect balance. While the dark-haired mayor flashed a down-to-earth, charismatic smile, his wife was more subdued.

But Holland read the blond-haired woman's demeanor like a book. Poppy purposely dimmed her light so her husband could shine brighter. But in her mind, everyone in the room was just lucky to have space.

A less polished version of the couple followed—the mayor's brother and his wife, Anna.

Gerard and Poppy briefly acknowledged the Tillbridge table and kept walking to the front of the room. Anna, however, came to a sudden stop. Her attention landed on Holland, and her eyes widened. She kept looking back as her husband nudged her along.

Rina murmured. "Well, Holland, it looks like you made tomorrow morning's news."

"Tomorrow?" Scott huffed. "Annoying Anna will post her version of the story as soon as she sits down. 'News flash—Holland Ainsley is in town to film the next one hundred *Shadow Valley* movie sequels…'"

Annoying Anna? Realization about who the woman was struck Holland. She was in charge of the town's online newspaper, the *Bolan Town Talk*. It was more like a gossip blog. During the filming of *Shadow Valley*, the woman had constantly hung around set, hoping to dig up her next story. And Anna had almost spoiled Chloe and Tristan's secret engagement.

Sitting at the Ashford table, Anna took her phone out of her purse and started tapping away.

Dread fell over Holland. Hopefully, the woman wasn't putting out wrong information about why she was there. The last thing she needed was people volunteering to be an extra. Maybe she should give Anna an exclusive to set the record straight. Sharing why she was in town could also help her find more leads on houses for the documentary.

Or it could backfire. Maybe, it was best to steer clear of pesky reporters who were willing to spoil special moments like engagements.

"Oh good. They're here." Rina smiled as she looked to the entrance of the dining room. "Who's that guy with them?"

Holland looked over her shoulder, and a small flush of heat crept into her face. *Oh crap...*

Chapter Four

Myles crossed the dining room with Tristan and Chloe.

Many of the people in the restaurant were staring at them. At first, he'd wondered if his blue Henley, jeans and casual lace-ups weren't dressy enough and he was out of place.

But Tristan was just as casual, and Chloe was also in jeans and a gray blouse that was almost the same color as her husband's shirt. Then it hit him.

It wasn't just that Chloe was an actress. The attractive Black couple's confidence was the main draw. Chloe and Tristan had an ease about them, and their bond was unquestionable.

Memories of being with Sydney came into his mind. Early in their relationship, they'd shared that same type of reassurance, believing they could conquer anything together. And they had…almost.

Myles let the recollection slip away as they reached a long table filled with people waiting for them.

"Hey, guys. Sorry for the wait," Tristan said, making sure Chloe was settled in her seat before taking his at the end of the table. "Everyone, this is Myles Alexander. Myles…"

Tristan pointed around the table, making introductions.

As Myles sat down, he exchanged nods and hellos with the friendly group.

Tristan's final introduction was the woman sitting almost across from Myles next to Chloe. "And this is Holland Ainsley. She's from California and also visiting Bolan for a few weeks."

Myles paused in putting the cloth napkin on his lap. She looked familiar. Like the girl who'd trespassed in his house. Maybe she was her older sister?

Holland met his gaze and smiled. "Hello."

As he looked into her light brown eyes, he realized it wasn't just a resemblance. It was her. And she wasn't a teenaged girl. She was a beautiful woman who just looked young for her age.

Believing she was one of the vandals that Tristan caught at the house, he'd just assumed she was in high school.

A server asked for his drink order, and Myles had to look away from Holland. But as the conversation flowed around him, he couldn't stop his gaze from drifting back to her.

Holland's tawny skin was flawless. Subtly applied makeup enhanced the delicate features of her face. The light in her eyes and her beautiful smile reflected genuine kindness, self-assurance and boldness.

In his mind, he remembered the vulnerability in her expression when he'd caught her in his house. The many layers to her personality raised his curiosity about her.

"Myles," Scott said. "What brings you to Bolan?"

Myles still wasn't sure what he was doing there, so he went with a basic answer. "I'm settling the sale on a house I own. It's on Oakview Road."

"Yes." Chloe smiled sweetly at her husband. "Not to be confused with the house that has murals on the walls."

"Sorry about that." As Tristan looked at Chloe, humor was in his apologetic smile.

Chloe pointed to Holland. "The apology needs to go to her. You sent my friend on a wild goose chase."

"Sorry, Holland," Tristan said. "The house Myles is working on has a decorative trim along the ceiling in one of the rooms. When Chloe said a house with art, I thought that's what she was referring to."

Holland shared a conspiratorial look with Chloe as she asked him, "But isn't confusing decorative trim with murals kind of like calling a donkey a horse?"

Tristan chuckled with amusement. "What? Not even close. Calling a donkey a horse is sacrilegious."

"And it might get you arrested in a few places,"

Mace added. "Wait—Holland, you were at Myles's house looking for murals?"

The attention shifted to Myles and Holland.

Her gaze connected with his and an electricity-like jolt waved through him.

As she took a sip of wine, she studied him over her glass.

Mesmerized by the sparkle in her soft brown eyes, he started to care less and less if she exposed him as *that* guy—a total jerk who'd thought she was a trespasser and kicked her out.

She set down her wineglass. "I was there, but Myles wasn't. We must have missed each other."

Why hadn't Holland set him up for the teasing he deserved? He wouldn't have blamed her if she had called him out on his behavior.

Torn between gratefulness and even more curiosity about her, he kept running the question through his mind.

As a server came to take their meal orders, Holland meeting his gaze clued in Myles that once again he'd been staring at her. Wait. Did she just give him a subtle wink? What did *that* mean? Was it her way of saying the secret of him being *that* guy was safe with her? Or did a lash just fall into her eye? He had no clue.

He hadn't really dated anyone since Sydney.

The conversation continued around him, but he half-listened, remembering how just thinking of his wife had once caused grief to loom like a large cloud of sadness inside him.

Even with all the time that had passed since then, it was still strange to just feel a ping that echoed and returned to silence. When he'd first experienced it, he'd felt guilty until he'd come to realize that holding onto grief wasn't the best way to remember Sydney. She wouldn't have wanted him to do that, and he'd never forget her. The life they shared would always be a part of him.

But he still hadn't mastered singlehood. It was like a foreign language he'd once known but had to learn all over again. And dating—his brother had convinced him to start venturing out there but he hadn't come across anyone he'd really connected with.

He wasn't looking for anything serious. Just someone to grab a meal with, meet for coffee one weekend or a drink after work. But there were so many expectations and rules, even for a basic, uncomplicated, friendly relationship.

With her beauty and confidence, Holland probably had the dating world all figured out.

A short time later the food arrived and everyone at the table was captivated by their entrees.

Myles knew of Dominic Crawford because of his cooking show, but he'd never had the opportunity to eat something prepared by him or any other celebrity chef.

Mouth watering in anticipation, he cut into his buttered whiskey steak, took a bite and almost moaned in appreciation. Sliced brussels sprouts mixed with spicy corn and bacon had automatically been paired with the meal, so he'd gone with it. Normally he didn't like the hard green balls that looked like baby cabbages. But these were delicious.

Across the table, Holland took a bite of her shrimp entrée. His gaze remained riveted on her plum-colored lips. As she slid the fork from her mouth and closed her eyes, the ecstasy on her face reminded him of something he hadn't had in a really long time— heart-pounding, never-wanting-it-to-end sex.

Holland took another bite, and as he watched her, his heart did pound.

But he shouldn't be having these thoughts about a woman he just met.

Tristan nudged him. "You're not eating. Something wrong with your steak?"

"Uh…" Myles dragged his gaze from her and gave himself a mental shake. "It's perfect."

The steak was great, but his mouth had suddenly dried out. He caught the attention of a server. "Could I have a beer, please?"

After the main entrée, there was a pause. Dessert would be served in a few minutes.

Some of the group stayed, while others got up, including Holland and Chloe.

Tristan turned to Myles. "When we talked earlier, you mentioned you were trying to schedule meetings with contractors. How's that working out?"

"I'm still looking for a plumber and a roofing company. And I also need a caretaker." Myles paused to take a sip of beer. "Peggy is great, but I need someone who can keep a closer eye on things until I can find a buyer for the place."

Tristan's brow rose. "So you're selling the house?"

The conversation with Dante played through Myles's mind. "Not right away. Once I nail down a few estimates, I'll decide if I'm going ahead with the remodel or selling it as is."

"I'm sure you'll find a buyer either way. If it'll help, I can give you the contact details for the contractors who built my house and ask around about a caretaker. And Scott used to work for his dad's plumbing company." Tristan pointed to the empty chair where Rina's husband had been seated. "Depending on the repairs, he might be able to give you a hand."

Myles hesitated. Tristan had already done a lot for him *and* welcomed him to dinner with his family. "I don't want to take up more of your time."

Tristan waved off the objection. "It's not a problem. Around here, we look out for our neighbors. I'll text you the info on the contractors and give Scott a heads up that you might want to talk to him."

A few good leads and an opinion on the plumbing would make the process easier. "I'd appreciate it. Thanks."

Tristan stood to find his wife, and Myles went outside to the deck.

Farther down, Holland stood with her back toward him, leaning her hands on the wide railing. She stared ahead, perfectly still.

Maybe he was disturbing her.

He turned to go back inside.

"You don't have to leave." Her voice reached Myles before he opened the door.

He'd needed air, partly because of her. Even when he hadn't been looking at Holland, he'd been aware of her presence across the table. Clearing his head before rejoining the group had been the plan.

But leaving would be rude. And honestly, he didn't want to.

As he reached Holland, the scent of her perfume, soft and sweet, wafted in the air.

He glanced at her at the same time she looked at him. She'd refreshed her lip color. The shade reminded him of a lush, ripe plum. Suddenly, a longing stirred inside of him to press his mouth to hers for a taste of their promising sweetness.

Not trusting himself to resist doing just that, he moved a fraction away from her. What was wrong with him? He usually had more control than this. And it wasn't like he'd never been around a pretty woman before.

Myles lightly gripped the railing. He released a breath and a small chuckle. "I really messed up this afternoon, didn't I?"

"Yes, you did." A hint of a teasing smile signaled she wasn't going to make this easy on him.

"But I have a good excuse."

"Oh really?" She turned toward him. "And what would that be?"

"A few weeks ago, a group of kids nearly started a fire in the back of the house. When I saw you, I thought…" Myles searched for the right words.

She laughed. "You thought I was there to cause trouble?"

"Yeah, something like that." He faced her. "But

you really should take some of the responsibility off my shoulders. You could have straightened out the situation by telling me who you were and why you were there."

"I was too afraid." Humor shone in her eyes. "You threatened to tattle on me to my parents."

A chuckle shot out of his chest. "Hold on. I'll confess that I shouldn't have jumped to the conclusion that you were a troublemaker, but thinking you were a teenager is an honest mistake. You could pass for one."

"Okay." She feigned acceptance with a shrug. "Since you put it that way, I'll admit to trespassing. Although in my defense, the door was open, and I called out to see if anyone was there. And I'll forgive you for assuming I was a fire starter.

Oh, she was a fire starter, all right. And if he wasn't careful, he just might get singed.

Laughter drifted from inside the restaurant. Almost everyone was back at their table.

Myles turned toward the large window. "They're a lively group."

"Yes, they are. And they're all really good people. How long have you known Tristan and Chloe?"

"I don't, really know them that well. Tristan was the one who chased the kids away when they set the fire." The stable owner's offer to help came into Myles's thoughts. "You're right about them being good people. Tristan is sending me leads on contractors, and he volunteered to help me find a caretaker. He's also going to talk to Scott about helping me. I'll definitely take the help if he agrees, but I hope he doesn't feel obligated to do it because Tristan's his brother-in-law."

"Brother-in-law?" The quizzical expression on Holland's face morphed to understanding. "Oh no, Scott's wife isn't Tristan's sister. She's his cousin."

"Really? As close as they are, I thought they were siblings."

She gave him an understanding look. "I did, too, when I first met them. But don't be surprised if you receive more offers for help. A lot of people in Bolan are generous in that way."

"That's so different from what I'm used to in New York. Sure, there's generous people, but they're more reserved and cautious."

She nodded in agreement. "It's different in LA, too. But in this town, once they accept you as part of their world, you're a member for life."

"That sounds welcoming and intimidating."

"That's an interesting way to describe it." She laughed. "The last time I was here was for the special screening of *Shadow Valley*. That was almost three years ago, but people still remember me."

Chloe had starred in that movie. In the parking lot, before coming into the restaurant, when Tristan had introduced his wife to him, it had taken Myles a minute to figure out why he'd recognized her.

"*Shadow Valley*," Myles said. "It was a good film. Wasn't it nominated for a few awards?"

Holland smiled slightly and glanced away. "Yes… it was."

For the first time that night, she seemed uncertain. Like she wasn't sure what to say. What was that about? Was there more to the story?

Inside the restaurant, a tall, thirtysomething man dressed in a charcoal chef's jacket and black pants walked up to the table with a pretty brown-skinned woman. She was similarly dressed in a lime green chef's jacket, and a matching band secured her dark locs.

Holland's expression animated. "Dominic and Philippa. The food was excellent. I have to tell them. Are you coming?"

"Go ahead. I'll be there in a minute." He needed to take a breath. Small town generosity, Hollywood celebrities, meeting Holland. It was all more than he expected.

She started walking away then paused. "Can I see it?"

Not sure how to respond, he cautiously asked. "See what?"

"The art Tristan described." Cocking her head to the side, she smiled. "It sounds like what I might be looking for—I'm researching old houses."

Myles almost told her it wasn't that interesting. But something about Holland made him want to see her again.

"Sure. No problem. Anytime."

"Great." She hurried inside.

Shoot. He'd forgotten to get her number. Or give her his. He'd do it before they left the restaurant tonight.

He wouldn't have pegged her for a researcher. Or

maybe she had a research job in the film industry. But she'd also mentioned attending a special screening for *Shadow Valley*. She *was* Chloe's friend. But something about her face looked familiar. Maybe she'd been in the movie with Chloe?

Myles watched through the window as Holland rejoined the group.

When the two chefs spotted her, they hugged her like an old friend.

She seemed to know everyone in the group well. And even though she was unattached, like him, she seemed to fit right in with the other couples. Holland *was* single, wasn't she?

The door opened, and Chloe beckoned. "Come meet Dominic and Philippa."

When he reached Chloe, he gave in to the urge to ask. "Holland's face seems familiar. Was she in *Shadow Valley* with you?"

"Holland wasn't in the movie." Chloe smiled but also seemed a little surprised by the question. "She directed it."

Chapter Five

Holland pulled up in front of Myles's house and butterflies erupted in her stomach.

She'd barely slept, excited about visiting him that morning. And also wondering if it was a good idea.

He was different from the guys that were part of her social circle in LA, but she'd enjoyed talking to him. He'd even been able to handle her sense of humor. A lot of guys couldn't. Instead of shutting down or backing away, he'd teased her right back. Experiencing that with him had been refreshing and attractive. And it had also led to her impulsive question.

But from what she'd noticed about Myles, he might appreciate company.

Sitting at the table in the restaurant, there were times when he'd drop out of the group's spirited conversation, and she'd glimpsed sadness in his eyes.

But when just the two of them had been talking on the deck, he'd transformed.

The memory of Myles releasing an honest laugh emerged. The wonderful, rich sound had danced over her skin.

Just like her, he could probably use more relaxing moments like that. Maybe while they were both in Bolan, they could meet up for coffee or lunch. As city dwellers, they could help each other understand the mysteries of small-town ways, and laugh again about their own feelings of intimidation and insecurity over them.

As she got out of the car with her backpack, Myles emerged from the house. Like her, he was casually dressed. But with his slightly scuffed tan work boots, his long legs encased in jeans and that gray T-shirt stretching across his broad shoulders and muscular chest, he gave off a hardworking-man vibe. The kind that said, if he took off his shirt in the middle of a physically demanding task, the sweat gleaming on his impressive torso wouldn't be for show.

Myles met her as she walked up the gravel driveway. "Holland—it's good to see you again."

His polite, reserved demeanor made her heart sink.

Something that had needled her conscience last night came to mind. When they'd traded numbers before leaving the restaurant, Myles *had* seemed more guarded than he had been talking with her on the outdoor deck.

She'd obviously misjudged the situation. Maybe he'd just said yes to her visiting out of some sense of obligation, because she was friends with the Till-bridges.

Setting aside disappointment, she forced a smile. "Hi. I appreciate you letting me stop by. I won't stay long. I know you're busy."

"You don't have to hurry. I'm not as busy as I'd hoped." A hint of frustration entered his tone. "The electrical contractor is running late, and another contractor I was supposed to meet today had to cancel."

"Oh no. I'm sorry to hear that. Would you prefer we didn't do this right now?"

"No, we're good." He walked toward the house. "Let's go see the decorative molding."

Holland stayed behind. "Is it just issues with the contractors that's bothering you? Please tell me the truth. You're acting differently toward me."

He turned back around and faced her. "I'm not treating you differently."

"Yes, you are."

Maybe it had been wrong to say it. But she didn't want to spend awkward minutes staring at the ceiling, pretending all was good if it wasn't.

Myles studied her a moment. "You seriously want the truth?"

"Yes, I do."

"Why didn't you tell me you were the director of *Shadow Valley*?"

Holland toed her boot in the gravel. She'd asked herself the same question lying awake last night. "I didn't want you to think I was trying to impress you. For me, one of the nice things about being in Bolan is that to most of the locals, I'm just another one of those Hollywood people. No one cares. I didn't want you to start acting weird around me."

"And you thought I might because I'm not from here." As he released a deep breath, some of the guardedness melted away. "Will you answer me truthfully?"

She nodded.

"Are you really here to see the decorative molding?"

"Yes…and no."

He looked into her eyes as if he was gauging her answer. A small smile tipped up his mouth. "I can accept that. I have sodas, a deli sub and chips in the house. There's enough for two. Do you want to join me?"

With the air now cleared between them, Holland couldn't hold back her own smile. "I'd love to."

A short time later, after she'd checked out the decorative molding, they sat out back on a blanket spread over the low, raised, wood deck. The weather made it a good day to sit outside and enjoy the breeze.

The large turkey and cheddar sub, a small bag of chips, and sodas were between them.

He gave her half the sandwich in a wrapper. Lettuce, tomato, green pepper, a dash of salt and pepper. Oil and vinegar instead of mayo. Just the way she would have ordered it for herself.

In between bites, Myles asked questions about her work. She told him about her production company. And she also explained the documentary she was researching, giving him the short explanation about houses and their stories.

He munched a chip. "So you're interested in the story the house can tell. Not so much about other people, but a particular experience that happened there."

"Exactly." Excited, she pointed at him. "You get it. You totally get it!"

His expression warmed with a smile. "What have you found so far?"

"There's a house with a spectacular wine cellar. The owner claims there are some interesting stories tied to it. I'm looking at it tomorrow. Then there's a house with a maze in the back of it. That might not be what I'm looking for, but I'll check it out. And there's a house just outside Bolan where a magician used to live."

"Those all sound promising. What's your time frame on project development?"

Story the house can tell...project development. The way Myles so easily interpreted what she was telling him made Holland's heart flip in her chest. "I'm here for two to three weeks now for research. I'll come back if I have to. As far as making the actual movie, it's not attached to another studio. It's all mine, so I can take my time to figure out the right story to tell."

"Why a documentary? *Shadow Valley* was such a big thing. I imagined making sequels would be your focus."

"I'm proud of the work everyone put into *Shadow Valley* and all the accolades, but…"

The love/hate pull she felt toward the film, which she could usually hide whenever she talked about the supernatural, sci-fi Western, emerged. She was forbidden from talking about sequels, but everything else was fair game.

She looked to Myles, who waited patiently for her to continue. "I've wanted to expand into other creative projects for a while, even before *Shadow Valley*. But sometimes you have to check a box before you can try other things."

He held out the small bag, offering her the last chip, but she let him have it instead. "So *Shadow Valley* was a strategic choice. A means to an end."

"Have you made choices like that with your career?"

"A time or two." He smiled. "It's not always easy. But you never know what's after try if you don't take a chance."

"I like that. It's the perfect definition. I hope you don't mind if I borrow it." She winked at him playfully. "But don't worry, I'll give you credit."

"It's not mine to claim." As he looked out at the trees, his smile faded. When he met her gaze again, the same sadness she'd witnessed last night briefly flickered in his eyes. "It's Sydney's."

Myles took in Holland's quizzical expression. He could wait for the question, or he could tell her who Sydney was to him. But either way he risked experiencing what she'd wanted to avoid by not telling him she was an award-winning director. That she would start acting weird around him if she knew his wife had passed away.

Some women he'd met had just stared, obviously uncomfortable with the revelation. Others ran the other way, as if the loss was somehow contagious. And then there were the ones who automatically jumped to the conclusion that he was so lonely, he'd jump on the offer of physical comfort without a second thought. On what planet was viewing him as desperate and themselves a sacrifice appealing? He had no idea. Sydney was probably laughing her butt off in those moments.

If Holland was going to treat him differently, he'd rather know that now. "Sydney was my wife. She passed away two and a half years ago."

Genuine empathy, and nothing else, shone on her face. "I'm so sorry."

Relief flowed through Myles. Holland hadn't gone tense or silent on him.

Usually, he left it at that, but her sincerity prompted him to say more. "She'd slipped on the stairs at her parent's house and bumped her head. I wasn't there when it happened. Everyone thought she was fine, but…she had a brain hemorrhage and died in her sleep."

Holland reached toward him and laid her hand on the blanket between them. "I can only imagine how hard that was for you and her family."

"It was." A hard swallow cleared his throat. "Sydney was a beautiful person. And she would have loved that you liked her advice."

"It's a good thing to remember. I'll make sure I give credit accordingly."

The companionable silence they shared for a few minutes was a breath of fresh air. Just like Holland.

Her hand still rested close to him on the blanket. A part of him wanted to reach out and lay his hand over hers. To feel her warmth.

Sydney slid her hand away and picked up her soda. After taking a drink, she looked out at the back yard. "Being outside like this is really nice. I haven't done anything like this in a long time."

"Really?" Skepticism filled his tone. "I'm sure someone has treated you to lunch at the beach or a park at least once?"

A look of contemplation came over her face. But then she grew more wistful. "No. Nothing spontaneous like this."

"The guy you're dating needs to get his act together."

A small knowing smile curved up her mouth as his unasked question hovered in the air.

He didn't want to read too much into her yes-no answer about why she was there. Catching up with her again for lunch sometime would be a nice break between trying to settle things with the house. But if she had someone special in her life, he wouldn't pursue it.

"I don't have a boyfriend at the moment." Holland shifted her attention to picking up a broken chip on the blanket. She dropped it on her empty sandwich wrapper. "Well as much as I'm loving this, I should get back to Tillbridge. I've got a video call with my office."

And he was expecting the electrical contractor. He'd almost forgotten about that. Myles glanced at his phone, surprised to see that it was almost time for the guy to arrive.

They'd been out there for over an hour? The time had flown by. And he could have kept talking to her.

They cleaned up together then went inside the house.

On her way out, she grimaced at the damaged pillar. "I feel terrible about this. I still can't believe that I moved one brick and the whole side practically collapsed. Are you sure you don't want me to pay for this?"

Before they'd gone outside for lunch, she'd asked him the same question, and he'd said no.

His answer hadn't changed. "I'm sure. The bricks were probably about to fall on their own. What you did brought it to my attention sooner."

Holland peered closer at where the mantel used to be on that side. "I could have sworn I saw something in this area."

"Like what?" he asked curiously, moving to stand beside her.

She shook her head. "I don't know. It could have just been a shadow. And if that was the case, I feel worse. I should just whip up a bucket of mortar and drop it off as housewarming gift."

Holland looked at him. Her smile was like the perfect day—sunny, cloudless and with a nice breeze.

He just wanted her to keep smiling at him. "Bring the mortar and a trowel, and it's a date." As soon as he said it, he wanted to snatch the words back. What he'd just said sounded like a pick-up line. A really bad one at that.

Thankfully, Holland laughed and shrugged. "I'll think about it. Knowing how to repair a fireplace might come in handy."

A few minutes later, as she headed out of the driveway, she honked the horn.

Mortar and a trowel? Smooth move, suggesting manual labor as a reason for her to stop by again. Why hadn't he just invited her to lunch?

Humor mixed with regret as he returned her wave. Yeah, he'd blown it with that last comment. She was never coming back.

Sydney...

In his dreams, Myles's wife sat at the table in the kitchen at the house where they'd once lived in Pennsylvania, drinking a cup of tea as she looked out the window. The view through the glass of the pristine backyard was vivid and lush.

As if sensing his presence, she turned to look at him. The soft sunlight shining through the window gave her straight brown hair and smooth naturally tanned skin an ethereal glow. A placid smile curved up her mouth.

In his dream, Myles hesitated in the archway, not

wanting to disrupt the quiet moment that had been part of her morning ritual. But he wanted to know why she'd bought him a house he didn't need.

Sydney's smile dimmed as she shook her head.

Chimes invaded the moment. As he partially woke up, he oriented himself to his surroundings.

He was lying on an air mattress in the upstairs bedroom of the house in Maryland. And the chiming sound was the ringtone he'd set for Dante.

Still half asleep, he reached down to the tarp covered floor, found his phone and answered it.

"Hey," Myles rasped out.

"Did I wake you?" Dante asked.

"Yep."

"Sorry. I thought you'd be up by now."

Remembering he had deliveries coming in that morning, his mind immediately cleared, and Myles opened his eyes.

Weak rays from the sun coming through the slats of the window shade turned the room a watery gray.

He sat up. "What time is it?"

"Just after six-thirty."

"I must have forgotten to set the alarm on my phone."

He'd started clearing dust and cobwebs from the loft. It wasn't as clean as the room he was in, yet, but it was an improvement. Once he'd finished, he'd been exhausted.

Thanks to the weather, the temperature of the house had been just right, not too hot or cold. He'd been comfortable sleeping in just a pair of sweatpants.

At least he'd kind of slept. Despite being tired, he'd kept waking up. And then, when he'd finally gotten to sleep, he'd started dreaming about Sydney.

Myles scrubbed his hand over his face. "Good thing you called, or I might have overslept. I'm expecting a delivery this morning. But why are you calling me?"

"You sounded off the other day. I'm just checking in. Are you okay?"

"Yeah, I guess." A vision of his wife flickered in Myles's mind. "But I did have a strange dream about Sydney."

"What do mean by strange? Did she say something to you?"

Myles recalled the expression on her face in the dream just before he'd awakened. Exasperated but indulgent—the same look she used to give him whenever she'd claimed he wasn't listening to her. That he was missing the point.

But she wasn't trying to tell him anything. It was just a dream. He just hadn't rested well because he wasn't sleeping in his own bed in New York.

The mattress dipped and wobbled as Myles got up. "No, it was strange because I haven't dreamed about her in a long time. I'm just overly tired."

"Which is why you should pump the brakes on rushing to get everything done. If you don't, you'll start resenting the house. Sydney definitely didn't want that for you when she bought it. Instead of turning it into a chore, why not just slow down—"

"I know. You've already made your point. I get it."

"But are you really hearing me?"

A loud thump came from the front of the house, and he peeked through the blinds.

Was it the dumpster and equipment he'd rented or the lumber and bricks? But the first delivery wasn't until eight. They must have gotten there early. But considering it was a Friday. Whoever it was may have gotten a jumpstart on their deliveries in anticipation of ending the day early.

That happened quite a bit with vendors when he was flipping houses.

The window, fogged from age, and condensation obscured the view. But he could make out a vehicle parked in the driveway.

Myles snagged a fresh gray T-shirt from his duffel against the wall and slipped it on. "The building supplies I ordered are here. I have to go."

"Building supplies? So you've decided to work on the house yourself?"

"I decided that since I'm going to be here for at least a couple of weeks, I could handle a few easy tasks."

"Good plan."

Myles stuffed his feet into his boots outside the bedroom door. The pleased tone in Dante's voice hadn't escaped him. "Uh-huh. I know what you're thinking, but that's not what's happening here. I'm just keeping busy in between waiting for the contractors to show up. I gotta go. Talk to you later."

As he clomped downstairs, the thumps continued.

The plan was to store the lumber and bricks out back, not in front. They would just have to move them.

Ready to issue instructions, he opened the front door.

Holland looked up from dragging a large tub from the top step onto the porch. She puffed out a breath. "Good morning."

Confused and speechless, he watched as she pushed it closer to the wall.

Smiling, she dusted her hands over the thighs of her jeans. "Wow. Carrying that from the car was harder than I thought."

Gray smudges streaked her long-sleeved pink pullover, and she had a couple on one of her cheeks, but the beige construction boots she wore appeared to be brand-new. Even in her disheveled state, she looked good.

And he was happy to see her. "What are you doing here?"

She grinned even larger as she spread her hands wide in a grand gesture. "I come bearing housewarming gifts. Mortar for your bricks."

Glancing to the right, he spotted another large tub, a smaller one and a plastic shopping bag with several cylinders and tubes.

She walked toward the supplies. "There were so many different kinds to choose from. And without knowing the specifics of the task, the guy at the store made sooo many recommendations. I decided to just buy some of each. And this..." She reached into one of the bags and took something out. "Ta-da!" she sang out as she handed it to him.

It was a trowel. Made for gardening, not repairing a fireplace.

"Uh, yeah, this is…" He glanced back at her. She looked so pleased with herself, he didn't have the heart to tell her.

Holland laughed. "I'm just messing with you. That expression on your face was worth it."

Reaching into the bag again, she pulled out the right kind of trowel for the job. "So… I'm ready, and I'm here until this afternoon. Put me to work. Oh wait. There's coffee and breakfast sandwiches in the car. And there's a forty-five-pound bag of mortar I need your help with."

Holland jogged down the steps. She was like a ball of energy bouncing to the car.

How many cups of coffee had she drunk already?

Her enthusiasm was so cute and infectious, he couldn't help but laugh as he clomped upstairs.

Holland said she was ready. But was *he* ready for her?

Chapter Six

Holland sat crossed-legged on the wooden slats of the back deck where she and Myles ate lunch yesterday,

Meanwhile, he oversaw the delivery of a large dumpster being positioned off to the side of the yard.

As she sipped her third hit of caffeine that morning from a cardboard cup, she relived the earlier moment of Myles opening the front door. She really had surprised him, and that made her happy. And so did the opportunity to right a wrong by contributing to the repair of the fireplace.

The other day, when he'd caught her trespassing, she'd been so distracted by him, she hadn't noticed the extent of the damage.

Yesterday, after getting an up-close look at it, she'd felt bad about causing him more work.

Myles telling her to show up with repair materials had been a joke. But during the ride home, the more she thought about it, showing up with a few pounds of mortar had felt like the right way to say sorry and assuage her guilt.

She just hadn't meant to buy so much of it. Tristan or even Scott might have been able to give her some guidance. But she didn't want to have to explain the trespassing incident.

Unfortunately, she hadn't kept discretion in mind when she was talking to Burke yesterday after the virtual meeting with her assistant.

He'd asked her to consider looking over a couple of scripts. She'd reminded him she was on vacation. And then she'd made a flippant comment about needing to get off the phone to buy mortar and a trowel for her date. That had extended the conversation and nearly caused her to hang up on him.

Burke had claimed she couldn't be seen with a guy on a date, and that she shouldn't risk getting involved with anyone until everything had blown over with Nash and Gina. She'd responded by telling him to mind his own business. He'd reminded her the whisper campaign was about *their* business, and her actions needed to line up accordingly.

As she recalled the slightly tense back and forth between her and her business partner, Holland's frustration renewed. She could have told him that Myles was just a platonic acquaintance, and her date wasn't really a date. But the way Burke had come across during their conversation, it was as if he wasn't even acknowledging the sacrifice she was making to safe-guard everyone's reputations, the future of the film, *and* their film company.

The truck that had delivered the dumpster drove from the backyard. Exhaust fumes momentarily filled the air, reminding her of being stuck in traffic back in LA.

She was on vacation. She should be free to relax and enjoy anything she wanted with whomever she wanted. Without restrictions. Except one. If she did decide to get involved with a guy, it would have to be a temporary thing. When she returned home, the production company's films and upcoming projects would once again become her priority.

Myles directed a guy driving a mini forklift filled with lumber to drop the load on the other side of the yard near the stack of bricks.

If she were going to get involved with anyone, temporarily, he would be the perfect choice.

They were both in town for only a few weeks. Once their time together was up, they'd go their separate ways. And even better, he wasn't from the area. She could return to Bolan in the future and not worry about the possibility of running into him and experiencing an awkward moment.

And the way he'd interacted with Chloe and Dominic, he wasn't easily starstruck. She'd had guys ask her to score them autographs from their favorite celebrities on the first date.

But those weren't the main incentives when it came to Myles and a fling. One of the most attractive things about him, aside from being able to talk to him, was that he was so real. No double talk, mansplaining, or attempts to impress her. And he was so…fit.

Myles rearranged a few of the bricks and straightened out pieces of lumber before covering them with a tarp.

Even from a distance, it was easy for her mind to fill in the flexing of his biceps, the bunch and play of muscle underneath his shirt, and his jeans molding to the tautness of his thighs.

In her mind, she conjured up the vision of him, turning and walking toward the deck. As his gaze held hers, a small, sexy smile curved up his mouth. The spark of want in his eyes spelled out intentions that even though Holland was imagining him coming to her, a flush of heat filled her cheeks.

In her daydream, she rose to her feet. As soon as Myles stepped onto the deck, they indulged in a long, deep kiss. One that continued as he backed her into the house.

On a reflex, her hand tightened around the coffee cup as she envisioned helping him take off his shirt. It was almost as if she could feel the warmth from his chest seeping into her palms as he lifted her and carried her toward the stairs.

Beeping from the forklift yanked her back to reality.

Whoa… Had she really just gone there? What was wrong with her?

As the guy drove the forklift from the yard, Myles

walked toward the deck. But he wasn't wearing the sexy smile she'd envisioned a few seconds ago. He was focused on the electronic tablet in his hands.

Holland drank coffee. It soothed dryness in her throat and help wash away the naughty daydream still lingering in her thoughts.

He joined her, sitting nearby on the deck. As he entered information into what looked to be a spreadsheet, a faint, clean woodsy scent emanated from him.

Mixed with the smell of her coffee, it was like an aphrodisiac, luring her in.

Holland caught herself swaying toward him, but not before he glanced up.

Myles raised his brow. "Something wrong?"

"Uh…no." Playing it off, she pointed at the screen. "Is that some sort of app?"

"Yes. It's for managing construction jobs, but it's also good for home improvements and other small projects."

"Do you do a lot of renovations or did you get an app just for this one?"

"My brother, Dante, owns a tech company that specializes in construction management software. This renovation is a good way to beta test components that were added to better separate home improvement tasks from business projects. I used to work construction, so that gives me an insight the tech gurus in the company, like my brother, might not have."

No wonder he was so confident in handling the remodel.

"That's nice your brother has you to test things for him."

"I'm kind of obligated. Otherwise, he won't pay me. I'm his operations manager." Myles gave her a wink. The smile that came with it was a close cousin to the one in her fantasy.

Pushing the thought from her mind, she shifted her gaze to the top of her cup. "You two must get along well to work with each other."

"We do." Myles tapped on the screen. "As long as he remembers I helped raise him and that he doesn't get to boss me around."

"Spoken like a true big brother."

"Sounds like you have one of your own."

"I do. His name is Ben, and we're opposites in every way. He's Mr. Regimented about everything. That's why the army suits him. He loves rules. He claims I only like to break them."

"No, you're not a rule breaker. But wait…" Feigning confusion, Myles pointed at her. "Aren't you the woman who broke into my house?"

"I didn't break into your house. The door was open."

"Are you sure about that?"

"Sort of." She laughed.

Chuckling he asked, "Are there any other rule abiding or rule breaking siblings in your family?"

"Oh, no. Just us. He was actually supposed to be an only child but, *surprise*."

"So that's why you're so good at surprises."

"Yes. Or at least I hope I am."

"You are." The small smile tipping up his mouth was an even closer cousin to the one in her fantasy.

Holland's heart flipped in her chest. Needing to do something other than just stare at him, she took a sip from her cup. Before lowering it, she licked a stray drop of coffee from the lid.

Myles's swift intake of breath brought her attention to him. His gaze was on her mouth.

The longing on his face ignited a spark of desire inside of her.

He shook his head, as if answering some internal debate and the yearning shadowing his face disappeared with a frown.

Clearing his throat, he glanced to the house and rose to his feet. "We should start working on the fireplace, since that's why you're here."

"Right… we should." Holland quickly stood.

Warring with disappointment, she walked into the house.

A part of her had wanted something more to happen like in her daydream. But she wasn't there to watch him lift heavy objects and fantasize about him taking off his clothes.

"Are you really here to see the decorative molding?"

That's what he'd asked her yesterday. She'd said yes… and no. And then she'd shown up on his doorstep bright and early with enough mortar to repair his fireplace ten times over.

Holland glanced at Myles. He faced away from her, staring toward the bricks and lumber in the yard.

She really did like him a lot, but even if she was seriously thinking of indulging in a fling with him, based on that last look she'd just witnessed on his face, he probably wasn't ready for anything past what they were doing. Having a mild flirtation and repairing his fireplace.

Holland went to one of the shopping bags she'd brought near the wall and took out a pair of work gloves. As she put them on, she accepted another truth. She hated to admit it, but Burke was right. Her personal life had to fall in line with the whisper campaign. On her list of priorities, Nash and Gina, the movie, and their film production company all came first.

Myles replayed the crestfallen expression he'd glimpsed on Holland's face before she'd walked into the house.

And the memory of her licking coffee from the lid of her cup.

It had taken all the discipline he could call up not to toss aside his tablet and satisfy his craving for caffeine courtesy of her lips. But caffeine wasn't what he really craved.

Her curves, her scent, they were more than just a little enticing. It would have been so tempting to lay her back on the deck to map out every one of her curves and find all the places where her perfume lingered on her soft skin.

As the vision started to form in his mind, he broke out in a sweat, and blood pooled below his waist.

A quiet intensity had existed between him and Sydney when they'd first met. And it was good.

Around Holland, he experienced straight-up need. He didn't trust it. Or himself around her.

But he couldn't stay outside forever. She was waiting for him.

After a few measured breaths, he walked inside and joined her by the fireplace.

He might not understand why he was so attracted to Holland, but renovations, repairs, he knew about that. He just needed to lean into it and stay focused.

Myles stepped slightly in front of her and pointed at the damaged section. "With all the broken and cracked bricks, it's probably best to just put in a new column. We'll take it down, starting with this one."

She peered closer. "You said the bricks are cracked? I don't see anything."

Holland stepped around the pile of bricks. Her shoulder brushed his as she took a closer look.

Goose bumps erupted on his arm. The light floral scent emanating from the curve of her neck captivated him.

Fighting the urge to press his lips to that very spot, he dragged his gaze back to the column. "They're hairline cracks. See that one there?"

Her foot bumped a pile of bricks on the floor, and she wobbled.

"Careful." He reached for her.

"What's that?" Holland leaned down and peered at the pile."

"What's what?"

"Right there under that brick." She stretched out her hand as if planning to move it.

"I'll get it." Myles hunkered down. "It's probably something the kids that broke in here left behind." Setting bricks aside, he unearthed a folded, wrinkled paper then handed it to her.

Myles poked around the other bricks. "Or if someone stuffed paper behind the column, that could explain why it was so weak."

"This does look like it's been here a while." Holland carefully unfolded the paper. A piece of blue fabric that fell out and she caught it in her hand.

As she glanced at the paper, her brow rose in surprise. "Oh…wow…this is interesting."

Chapter Seven

Myles stood. "What is it?"

"It's a letter." She briefly looked at the back of it. "But there's no name or address on it."

"What's it say?"

"I think it's a breakup letter."

"Really?" He accepted the note from her and read it aloud.

Dear B,
I'm leaving. After seeing you this afternoon as a bridesmaid, all I can think about is you walking down that same aisle as a bride. Like I told you at the reception, I can't watch you marry him. I know it's about pleasing your family, but we've been right for each other since that day we met at the flea market fair and rode the roller coaster together. I want everyone to

*know how I feel about you, and it hurts. You
tore your dress when you ran away from me
in the courtyard at the church. A piece of it
was stuck to one of the rosebushes. I've been
holding on to it, but I can't keep it any longer.
It just reminds me that I'm losing you. We belong together. Run away with me.
L*

"Huh." Myles chuckled. "Whoever L was, the guy
clearly had it bad."

"He sure did." Holland stared at the letter and the
torn fabric with lace. "I wonder if she ran away with
him? Someone around here might know."

He understood the gleam in her eyes. "This letter and the story behind it fit with the theme of the
documentary you're making."

"It could." Her expression turned hopeful. "Would
you mind if I hold on to the letter for a few days and
look into it?"

The letter meant nothing to him. But he could see
she was eager to learn more about it. He handed her
the paper. "Keep it for as long as you want."

"Are you sure? Depending on how old it is or who
wrote it, this could be valuable."

He could practically feel the excitement bouncing
off of her, as if she couldn't wait to dive headfirst into
the mystery. That was understandable considering
it could fit with her project. He'd felt some of that
exuberance, too, years ago when he flipped houses.
He couldn't take that away from her.

"I'm sure."

"Thank you!" Enthusiasm lit up her face, and his chest swelled a little. "I'll search the records for the house first. Once I have a name, I can probably find out about the families who lived here. A name might match up."

"Then what?" he asked. "That letter was probably hidden for a reason."

"That did cross my mind, too," Holland acknowledged, glancing down at it. "I'm just hoping there's a happy ending to the story."

Caution prompted him to ask. "And if there isn't?"

Her expression sobered as she folded the paper back up. "Then I'll have to tread lightly."

Setting the letter aside, Myles and Holland loaded bricks into the wheelbarrow that had been delivered with the equipment he'd rented. They'd both wondered if there were more letters buried under the pile, but so far, nothing had emerged. For some reason, he felt almost as disappointed as Holland was about that.

He eventually stopped adding bricks to the wheelbarrow. "I'll take this load out before it's too heavy. The ramp I built for the porch can only take so much weight."

As he adjusted the gloves on his hands, he anticipated a response from Holland, but she didn't say a word. Instead, she kept loading bricks. From her expression, he could tell she was mulling something over.

"Holland…" He laid his gloved hand on hers, and

she looked up at him. "Did you hear me? I said I'm taking this load out."

"Oh, sorry." She brushed her gloved hands together, wiping off the dust, clearly still lost in her thoughts.

Most likely her mind was on the letter.

"You should go downtown and start researching."

"No." She laid her hand on his arm and his heart thumped a hard beat. "I'm here to help you."

As she took her hand away, her warmth lingered. And distraction still shadowed her expression.

His concentration wasn't fairing any better than hers, and distraction and repair work wasn't a good mix.

"I don't mind doing it on my own." He tipped his head toward the door. "Go."

Holland was already taking off her gloves. "Are you sure you don't want me to help you finish this part?"

"Yeah. I'm sure."

As she backed away, she said playfully, "Don't have all the fun without me. And definitely call me if you find more letters. I'll be back tomorrow."

"I promise to let you know if that happens." He smiled at her. "And call or text me if you find something."

She grinned back. "I will."

Holland left, and he finished clearing away the bricks on the floor. When he was done, he grabbed his safety glasses and a particle mask from his toolbox then started chiseling bricks from the broken column.

Usually, methodical tasks like this cleared his mind, but his thoughts kept swaying back to Holland…and Sydney.

When he and his wife first met, she'd been twenty-two years old. Having grown up in a privileged family, she'd been carefree.

Being responsible and setting a good example for Dante had been his focus. And that had meant always thinking twice before doing anything, including getting involved with her. His reserved nature had driven Sydney nuts.

Six months into their relationship, he and Sydney were clearly committed to each other. But he'd insisted they wait another six months before getting engaged and a year after that to get married.

Mr. Wait-and-See. That's what she'd teasingly called him.

After she'd passed away, he'd gone round and round in his head, wondering if he should have been less cautious…about a lot of things. And not just waited and waited and waited.

Myles hammered against the chiseling tool he was holding against one of the bricks.

It broke away from the pillar and crumbled on the floor.

Myles shoulders sank with the release of a harsh breath. But that was the past. What about now? Was his remorse over waiting on so many things when it came to him and Sydney controlling his actions with

Holland? Was it tempting him to jump into unknown territory with her before thinking twice? That wasn't smart. He'd just met her a few days ago.

And he didn't come to Bolan to get involved with anyone. He was here to sell this house. Checking *done* on every project that needed to be completed was his priority.

And Holland was in town to make her documentary.

But the part of him that remained unconvinced that he shouldn't give into his longings when it came to Holland gnawed at his reasoning.

Two days later, the gnawing had transformed into frustrating disappointment.

Holland wasn't coming back to help him.

The records department in Bolan was still in the process of adding files into a new computerized system aka "The Stone Age".

As he recalled his conversation with her day before yesterday, Myles swept brick dust and debris from the now cleared spot where the old column used to be,

The ones for his house hadn't been entered yet. She was planning to spend the weekend searching through documents that were out of order, trying to find the ones for his house. She was that dedicated to cause.

And he was spending the weekend trying not to think about her. That was close to impossible with the tubs of mortar she'd bought sitting across the room. They kept reminding him of her showing up on his doorstep the other morning and how cute she'd looked. And how much he'd been looking forward to seeing her again.

It didn't make any sense. He'd just met her. Like a hamster on a wheel, once again, like it had for the past two days, the "why" question ran like hamster on a wheel in his mind.

Dante was right. He did overthink a lot of stuff.

His stomach growled.

Food. He didn't have to over think that.

The other night at Pasture Lane, Chef Philippa had mentioned how popular the restaurant's food van was becoming at the Tillbridge Stable Indoor Horse Arena. Hadn't he noticed a sign for the building when he'd driven to the restaurant for dinner? And Tillbridge was closer to him than downtown.

After changing into a clean beige T-shirt upstairs, he snagged his wallet and keys from his duffel and headed to out. EAT

It was a good weather for a Sunday drive. On the way to his destination, the view of trees and open fields, along with listening to a radio station that played an upbeat mix of R&B, pop, and hip hop, lifted his mood.

On the same road as Tillbridge Horse Stable and Guesthouse, just as he'd remembered, Myles spotted a sign. Instead of turning into the parking for the guesthouse, it directed him to keep going.

Farther down, he spotted an entrance and a blue and white sign for the Tillbridge Stable Indoor Horse Arena.

In front of him, a black truck with a horse trailer

hitched to it made the turn into the half full parking lot, and he did the same.

The truck with the trailer drove straight ahead, passing the large sandstone-colored building on the left.

On the opposite end of the parking lot, a lime green vehicle, taller and longer than the average van, sat parked off to the side.

At a little after one in the afternoon, the van was fairly busy. Most of the dozen or so small folding tables and chairs arranged in front of it were occupied.

Myles parked in a spot near the van and got out.

The savory smell of food in the air confirmed he'd made a good choice coming there for lunch.

After a short wait in line to order and pay for his food, he carried a bottle of soda, plastic silverware, and a cardboard box loaded with honey habanero wings and fries to an empty table.

As soon as he took a seat, he dug in. The perfect blend of sweetness and spicy peppers woke up his taste buds.

Tristan calling his name made Myles look up.

The co-owner of Tillbridge strolled over to his table. "Hey, how's it going?"

"Good." Myles glanced at the sauce on his fingers. "I'd shake your hand, but…"

Tristan laughed. "I understand. Didn't mean to interrupt you."

"You're not. Have a seat."

"Are you sure? I'm dusty. I've been helping get horses settled in stalls at the arena."

"You're good."

As far as Myles was concerned, the smudges of dirt on Tristan's navy Tillbridge T-shirt, boots and jeans were a sign of hard work. He had nothing but respect for that.

Tristan pointed to the van. "I need to grab something. I'll be back."

A short time later, he returned with a bottled water, a small cardboard food box and a plastic fork. He put everything on the table, along with his phone. Anticipation was written on his face as he opened the box. He took a bite and smiled in contentment. "This lemon cobbler is exactly what I needed."

"Is that all you're eating?"

"I grabbed a sandwich earlier, but I didn't have time for dessert. I've been hard charging all day."

Myles pointed at the building. "What's going on at the arena?"

"An outside group is hosting a beginner's riding clinic."

As they ate, Tristan told him about the competitions and other special events coming up.

"You have a lot happening," Myles said.

"We do." Tristan nodded and blew out a breath. "But busy is good. What about you? I'm sure you've got your hands full with the house. How's that going?"

"The list of companies you sent me really helped. I have contractors starting work next week. But I've decided to do some of the work myself."

"So you might be here a while longer?" Tristan asked.

At this point, Myles couldn't rule that out. Especially if he wanted the work done fast and right.

"Possibly." He closed his empty food box and nudged it aside. "There's a lot to get done. The only space that doesn't need a ton of work is the dining room."

Tristan released a wry chuckle. "That's where the decorative molding and not the art is located, right?"

"That's the place."

"Chloe mentioned Holland thought your house could be helpful to her research. Was Holland able to link up with you about that?"

"She was…"

Myles hesitated to say more, especially about finding the letter. She might have preferred keeping the information under wraps until they knew more about it.

Tristan's phone buzzed with a text, and he checked the screen. "Mace doesn't have to work tonightm after all. He wants to hang out. If you need a break, you should join us."

Getting out of the house and blowing off steam, Myles was definitely up for that. "Sounds good to me. What's the plan?"

"He wants to go to the Montecito. It's a local bar and restaurant just outside of town."

A stable hand approaching the eating area flagged down Tristan.

Tristan looked back to Myles. "Can you hold on a minute?"

"Sure."

As the co-owner of Tillbridge got up to meet the worker, Myles's phone rang.

The number on the screen was Holland's. Curiosity about her progress with the letter and a gladness he couldn't deny prompted him to pick up. "Hello."

"Hey, Myles. How's the fireplace going?" She sounded down.

"The old bricks are gone. I'm ready to put down the new ones. What about you?" He toyed with a towelette packet he hadn't used on the table. "How's the search going. Any luck?"

"None yet. Which means that right now, you might actually be the only one who can prove you own that house."

"I have a copy of the deed in New York."

"Good." She sighed. "Because this place is a mess."

Clearly the wind had been taken out of her sails… and that bothered him. She'd been so enthusiastic about the search earlier. He'd honestly hoped she'd find something. "So what's next?"

During the silence, he reined in hope about the possibility that Holland might say she was coming by the house.

"I'm heading to the guesthouse. I have to check in with my assistant, and I have a script to read." Her tone brightened. "But I did get a bit of promising news today."

"Really? What?"

"The guy who owns the maze house called. He said I could come by late this evening. I wish we could meet earlier. The house is outside of Bolan in the middle of nowhere. And it's mostly backroads. It'll probably be dark when I'm heading back."

He stopped toying with the packet. "Are you going?"

"I should. Otherwise, I might not get another chance. He says he has a busy schedule. This may be a perfect house for my documentary. It's at least a hundred years old."

Traveling on isolated roads in the middle of nowhere to see a backyard maze, owned by a guy she didn't know? Myles couldn't stop his city sensibilities from kicking into overdrive.

But she could be aware of all he was thinking and perfectly equipped to handle any situation that might happen on her own.

"Well…be careful." He didn't want to be overprotective, but he couldn't hold back his concerns. "What about Chloe, Rina or Zurie? They probably know the area. Maybe one of them can go with you?"

"Chloe is out of town. And it's so last minute, I'm sure Rina and Zurie are busy. I'll be fine."

Just as he was about to suggest she text him on the way there and back, Holland asked, "Do you have time to go with me? I can pick you up."

He released a small breath of relief. "What time do you want to leave?"

"About six."

"I'll be ready."

Just as they said their goodbyes, Tristan sat down at the table. "So, about the Montecito…"

Myles wanted to hang out with the boys but riding

along with Holland was important. And he couldn't deny, he'd missed her. "About that…"

Holland headed east like the map app on her phone instructed.

Myles was beside her in the front passenger seat. Since she'd last seen him, he'd changed into a fresh shirt and a pair of black jeans. He looked really good…like he was going somewhere special. Had he dressed up for her…or did he have other plans?

As Holland contemplated being nosey and asking him, she noticed Myles frowning at the screen of his phone.

"Is something wrong."

"Yes and no." He chuckled wryly. "I'm still beta testing our company's app. Right now, it's pointing out what I already know—I screwed up."

"How?"

"I thought the plumbing could wait a little longer. Before you picked me up, I was in the shower when a pipe disconnected. Water was spraying all over the place, and I had to get to the shutoff valve with shampoo stinging my eyes." He winced.

A vision of rising steam and him in the shower with water raining down on his bare torso arose in her mind.

She almost drifted off the road but caught herself and steered the car straight. "You should have stayed and taken care of it. I would have understood."

"No. I'm good. I wanted to come with you."

As she briefly glanced over at him, the sincere

concern in his gaze along with something else she was afraid to read too much into released giddiness inside of her.

She was glad he agreed to come along. While she was searching through documents in the records office, her thoughts had kept going to him. Wishing he was there with her. Just to keep her company, of course. Friends. That was all they could be because of her situation.

A seed of glumness started to sprout, and she tamped it down. Changing the subject, she added, "I learned the hard way about knowing where the water cutoffs are for the pipes. Years ago, when one burst in the kitchen of my apartment, I didn't. And it happened literally two minutes before I had to leave to make it on time for a major go-see."

"What happened?"

With very few cars and lots of open road ahead, Holland inched up to five miles over the speed limit, then put the car on cruise control. "Luckily, one of my roommates came back from her audition. She understood why I had to leave and took over solving the problem."

"So you were an actor?" he mused. "Or I guess you still are, even though you direct? How does that work?"

"No, I modeled for a few years."

Myles's eyes lit with interest. "So model to film director…how did that switch happen?"

Holland went with the shorter version of the story. "My brother, Ben. I'd started modeling when I was sixteen. Once I turned eighteen, I moved to New York. Contrary to what some people believe, it's not just dressing up to take pictures."

"I can imagine there's a lot of discipline involved—competing for jobs, staying at the top of your game physically. And, I can imagine, mentally."

"Exactly." She hadn't expected him to say that. Most people didn't factor in that part and only saw the perceived glamour.

Holland continued, "Ben didn't have anything against me being a model. He just wanted me to have a backup plan. Drama club, writing stories, etc. I'd been involved in those things, too, growing up, and I loved it. So, fast forwarding my story a few years—after receiving a scholarship, lots of hard work, some really fabulous mentors, and one of my independent films taking off early in my career, here I am. And I'll never take it for granted."

She glanced over and saw him smiling at her with a pensive almost awestruck look on this face. "What?"

"Honestly, I'm not sure what to say. Telling you that's impressive or amazing might sound condescending."

"Depends on who it's coming from and if they mean it."

"I think you're impressive and very amazing. And I mean it." His gaze held the same look she'd been afraid to interpret just a minute ago.

Her heart flipped. "Thank you." Around Myles she genuinely felt amazing.

"A busy career probably hasn't left you much room for a personal life?"

Her years with Nash ran through her thoughts… along with the Nash and Gina situation now. She didn't want to ruin the moment by bringing any of that up.

She focused on the road. "No. It hasn't."

A few miles later, she parked in the gravel driveway of a single-story house with a wraparound front porch. The home wasn't fancy—white siding with decorative black shutters. Wood latticework covered the foundation. A small patch of grass and one small tree made up the front yard.

Across the road was a field surrounded by a wire fence and another house in the distance.

A truck was parked off the road, and man wearing a ball cap and brown coveralls was working on the fence.

Myles pointed to the house. "How old did you say this place was?"

"It's supposed to be at least seventy-five to one hundred years old."

He released a derisive snort. "The only thing that old about this place is the warped frame whoever stuck the vinyl siding on. Who owns this?"

"An older couple used to own it until a few months ago. Chet, the guy who's meeting me, is the property manager."

Myles was right. The house did look like it was leaning to the right a little. And it also didn't quite look like the one she'd seen online. If she was at the wrong house again… But she'd googled the house two months ago, so it was possible that work could have been done on it since then. Hopefully the maze was worth it, and she hadn't dragged Myles away from an important plumbing issue for a wild goose chase.

They climbed the steps to the porch. Not seeing a doorbell, she knocked on the door.

Seconds passed. No one came.

The blinds were closed on the windows, so they couldn't see if anyone was inside.

Holland took her phone from the front pocket of her backpack. She laid the pack on a wood bench positioned under one of the windows. "I'll give him a call."

Myles turned toward the stairs. "While you're doing that, I'll take a look in the back."

"Okay, thanks." She dialed the number. Hopefully the guy was on his way.

As the number rang, Holland paced. The planks in the porch felt kind of springy.

Suddenly the wood collapsed under her.

Chapter Eight

Holland's scream reached Myles as he was halfway to the backyard. Fueled by instinct and adrenaline, he ran back down the side of the house.

He reached the front, ready to defend her from whatever was trying to cause her harm.

Where was she? Had someone dragged her into the house?

Just as he was about to call out her name, he saw the gaping hole in the porch. *No!*

He hurried up the stairs, desperate to get to her as fast as possible. But then he made himself slow down, inching closer to the edge of the jagged opening.

Holland was a lot smaller than him, and the porch had given way. He didn't want to fall through or, worse, land on her.

He stretched out on his stomach, better distributing his weight, as he looked down.

Holland wasn't just a couple of feet below him but in a deeper hole in the ground. And as hard as he tried, he couldn't reach her. He could see her legs on top of the broken planks. But she wasn't moving.

"Holland… Holland," he called out. *Please…*

His silent prayer was answered.

Relief poured through him as she slowly sat up on the planks. She could move her legs and arms. That was a good sign. And it didn't look like she'd fallen into a sinkhole. The dirt appeared loose, but it wasn't caving in.

Holding the back of her head, she looked upward. "Myles…" Her voice was soft, and she seemed dazed.

"I'm here…it's going to be okay." He swallowed hard, forcing himself to stay calm. "Is the ground solid enough for you to stand on?"

She glanced around. "I—I think so."

"Go ahead and try."

Holland got to her feet, and he released part of a breath that had been sitting in his chest.

"Everything okay?" An older man with gray hair and a short beard hurried across the yard. "I heard a scream but didn't see anyone."

Myles recognized him as the man who'd been working on the fence. "My friend's fallen through the porch into a hole. I can't reach her. Do you have a rope or a ladder?"

"I've got a ladder at the house. My son can bring it. He's less than ten minutes away."

As the man made the call, Myles turned his attention back to Holland. Even standing, she was too far down for him to pull her out. "What's happening?" she asked.

"We're getting you help," he reassured her. "Just hang in there, all right?"

She nodded weakly.

"My son is on his way," the man told him a moment later.

Holland had her phone and was using the flashlight app to look around.

"Myles..." Unease was in her voice. "I think something's down here." She picked up a broken plank, holding it like a weapon and backed up.

The panic on her face sent another spike of helplessness through him. The ladder was coming, but he couldn't wait. He'd known in his gut that coming here had been a mistake. Why hadn't he listened?

"Move closer to the side. I'm coming down." Myles maneuvered to a sitting position, then jumped.

As soon as he landed at the bottom, he glanced around but didn't see anything moving in the shadows, only what looked to be piles of sandbags. What had she seen before? Rats, a snake or some other creature, maybe?

Myles reached for Holland. He gently took her by the shoulders. "How badly are you hurt?" He looked at her from head to toe.

"I scraped my arm." She glanced at the injured area.

Grateful she hadn't suffered more serious injuries, he wrapped an arm around her shoulder and brought her close.

Leaning into him, she added, "And I hit my head… I felt dizzy a minute ago, but I think I'm okay now." She touched near the back of her scalp.

Sydney… When she'd fallen and hit her head, she'd thought she was okay.

Renewed panic seized him and worked to keep his fears in check. Releasing a slightly unsteady breath, he kissed her temple.

The bearded man and a younger guy looked down at them. Myles breathed a sigh of relief that help had arrived.

"Are you ready for the ladder?" the man's son called down.

"Yes." Myles beckoned as he released Holland. "Lower it."

Moments later, the ladder came down, and Myles helped position it.

Holland went up first, and when she got closer to the top, the two men helped lift her out. Myles followed.

Reaching the top, he looked for her. Spotting her sitting on the bench, he immediately went to Holland, dropped down beside her and cupped her dirt-smudged face.

Her eyes grew bright as if she was about to cry.

He understood why. It was a natural reaction. Adrenaline was starting to fade, and the reality that she was safe had started to sink in.

"You're okay, Holland. I got you."

As she leaned against his shoulder, he took a full breath. Her scent, the warmth of her skin was his own assurance that the crisis was over. He could have lost her. Holland meant something to him. He had an opportunity to explore what that meant, and he wasn't going to waste time waiting or second guessing how he felt about her anymore.

A younger version of the old man came over to them. "I'm Roy. I used to be an army medic. I've got a first aid bag. I can clean up those cuts if you like."

Myles answered, "We'd appreciate that."

"Thank you," Holland whispered.

The father and son walked back to the truck.

She took a shaky breath. "First I knock down a fireplace, and now I fall into a hole. I'm either a klutz or a walking version of bad luck."

He tipped up her chin and looked into her eyes. "No, you're not."

Embracing the promise he'd just made to stop waiting, he gave in to the impulse and pressed his mouth to hers.

Holland's full lips were soft and pliant. He didn't want the kiss to end.

When he did, Holland looked stunned, but she didn't move away.

"I know that was bad timing, but I just needed to do it." He withdrew his hand.

Holland cupped his cheek. Smiling softly, she met his gaze. "Thank you. I needed that kiss."

She urged him to lean in. Their lips met for a long, lingering kiss that released a potent mix of relief and gratitude, heat and want. Holland parted her lips, but he eased back, afraid that once he got a taste of her, he wouldn't be able to stop.

Roy returned with his bag, and Myles got up.

While Roy tended to Holland, Roy Sr. gave Myles his opinion about Chet.

"I think he's a con man. The Colsons—they're the older couple that used to live here—had to be moved into a nursing home a few months ago. The house was in such bad shape, it was starting to sink down on one side. We expected whoever bought the place would tear it down. But when Chet showed up as the new owner, he just rebuilt over the dilapidated frame."

The pile of sandbags underneath the house. Had that been the guy's attempt to prop the damn house up? Myles didn't even want to go there in his mind.

"Owner?" Myles glanced to Holland. She winced as Roy checked the injury near the back of her head. "He told Holland he was the property manager."

Roy Sr. jabbed his finger in the air. "That's what I mean by con man. He never gave a straight answer. He even told my son he had to get the work done on the house for an important documentary. He claimed he was about to make a lot of money because of it."

As the picture of the type of man Holland had been dealing with became clearer, anger on her behalf seethed inside of Myles.

The older man was still on a roll. "And the maze that used to be out back, my son and I started taking care of it after the Colsons couldn't. It had garden benches and trellises. It was beautiful. But Chet mowed it down and put some cheap, gaudy imitation with blinking lights in its place..."

Later on, sitting in the reception area of the emergency room, waiting for Holland, Myles continued to think about the conversation.

No one had seen Chet in a while. The father and son had said they hoped Holland would sue the man if he showed back up. In the meantime, Roy Sr. planned to contact the authorities. If the house was a danger, it needed to come down.

Myles agreed with them on all counts, but in the end, it was up to Holland. But right now, she just needed to focus on herself.

Roy Jr. had said she should get checked out by a doctor. And he'd backed him up on that suggestion.

The ER wasn't busy. She'd been taken to an examination bay almost as soon as they'd walked in. The doctor wanted to have a head scan done and take a few X-rays.

Tired from moving loads of bricks that morning, Myles sat back in the black chair. He was mentally hyped and emotionally exhausted at the same time. He closed his eyes.

A vision of Holland lying in the hole rose up along with a remnant of the fear he'd felt when she didn't move right away. And the helplessness when he couldn't get her out. She'd been down there alone.

Myles scrubbed his hand down his face. One thing was for sure, he wasn't leaving her alone after they left the hospital. He got up and started to pace, letting his mind skip to the much better memory of kissing Holland. And how good it had felt to hold her and know she was okay.

If she let him, he was going to hold her all night.

Long hours later, he walked with Holland to her suite at the Tillbridge guesthouse.

Soreness in her right hip had kicked in, and she was moving slower than usual.

Natural fatigue coupled with a mild pain reliever had also started to take effect.

She'd been fortunate not to have a concussion. Just some cuts, bumps and bruises. The ER doctor had told her to take it easy for a day or two. He'd also suggested it wouldn't be a bad idea to have someone look after her tonight as a precaution.

Myles already knew he wasn't spending the night at the house worrying about her. Holland hadn't objected to him staying with her. On the way to the guesthouse, he'd swung by his place and packed his smaller duffel bag.

While he'd been waiting for Holland in the emergency room, he'd called Tristan to let him know why he wouldn't be joining him and Mace at the Montecito that night as they'd planned. That had led to a succession of calls and texts from Zurie, Rina, and, of course, Chloe. They all cared about Holland. He'd assured them he'd look after her.

Holland blew out a breath. "It feels like where I have to go is miles away."

The door to the suite was at the end of a blue-carpeted hallway.

"I can carry you?"

"No. You're already carrying our bags."

"No worries." He propped them against the wall. "Just think...the quicker I get you there, the sooner you can rest."

From the expression on her face, she was more than a little tempted.

Before she could talk herself out of it, he lifted her arm over his shoulder and braced his hand on her back. "Hold on to me." Being as gentle as he could, he picked her up as she wound both arms around him.

"You okay?" he asked, settling her in her arms.

"Yes." As he strode down the hall, she laid her head on his shoulder. "Thank you."

"You're welcome." Carrying her definitely wasn't a hardship.

Chapter Nine

In the suite, Myles took Holland to the blue couch in the living room.

Just like in her fantasy earlier that day sitting on his back deck, he'd carried her with little effort. If she hadn't felt like a truck had mowed her down, she would have enjoyed it more.

A slight twinge from the bruise on her hip made her suck in a small breath filled with his masculine scent. Even in pain, awareness awakened inside of her.

He studied her with concern. "Are you okay sitting here until I get the bags."

"Uh-huh. Go ahead. I'm fine." As he walked back out, she slipped off her shoes then sank slowly back on the couch.

The soft glow from two floor lamps lit up the space.

The living room was decorated in soothing hues of soft white, blue and sage that inspired a sense of relaxation. The corner bedroom with a spa bath echoed the same colors. A second bedroom had been turned into a charming office with a couch and white oak desk.

The kitchen and dining area were equally welcoming, with windows and a sliding glass door providing views of the surrounding pastures and the courtyard with trees below.

It was the perfect place to be right then. Having Myles there made it even better. Since the incident at the maze house, he'd *been sweet, gentle and strong at the same time. It was so soothing. She appreciated him so much after all she'd just been through.*

She closed her eyes and the past few hours, from falling in the hole to now, flashed in her mind like scenes from a horror movie.

She'd overheard some of the things Roy Sr. had said about Chet. Now that she thought more about it, something had felt a little off about the property manager/owner when she'd talked to him on the phone. The way he'd tried to upsell the maze, he'd sounded like a cheesy salesman. But she'd been excited to see it and had labeled him as eccentric. Boy had she been wrong.

What if she hadn't asked Myles to go with her? Would she still be stuck in that hole? Holland shuddered at the thought and her head started to throb. She stretched out on the couch.

When Myles had told her he wanted to watch over

her tonight, she'd been so grateful. But even if she had said no, she got the feeling he would have still found a way to do it. He was really concerned about her...

"Holland...wake up."

As Myles gently shook her, she lifted her heavy eyelids and focused on his face. She must have dozed off.

He gave her a soft smile. "You can't sleep here. This is my spot for the night. I'll help you to the bedroom."

If lying in bed wasn't a more comfortable proposition, she might have argued with him. She didn't want to move. "Okay." As they walked from the couch to the corner bedroom, she felt steadier with his hand resting on her back. "You know, you don't have to sleep on the couch."

"I..." Myles hesitated, appearing conflicted.

She deciphered the look on his face and realization cut through her grogginess. He thought she'd meant he should sleep with her in the bedroom.

Holland quickly clarified, pointing to the door between the guest bathroom and the kitchen. "The office—the couch pulls out into a bed. It'll probably be more comfortable. "I think there's a set of spare sheets in the guest bathroom closet. I'll look."

A hint of embarrassment flickered across his face. "Oh...yeah, that would be more comfortable. Don't worry about the sheets, I'll find them."

Crap. She hadn't meant to make him feel uncomfortable. It wasn't that she didn't want him in her bed. But how could she explain that without making things more awkward?

He urged her to keep walking.

In the bedroom, the welcome sight of the large king-size bed with fluffy pillows pulled a sigh of anticipation out of her. But she was way too grungy to just slip between the sheets.

Myles set her backpack on the dresser against the wall. As if reading her mind, he said, "Why don't I draw you a bath? It'll help with the soreness. While you're relaxing, I can make you something to eat."

She wasn't hungry. He'd gotten her chicken nuggets at a fast-food place on the drive from the hospital so she could take a prescribed pain pill.

But sitting in a large tub filled with nice warm water…she was relaxing just imagining it. "I'd love that. Thank you."

Myles went into the spa bath and the sound of water running in the tub echoed.

Remnants of what looked to be a cobweb on the leg of her jeans raised distaste. She wanted out of her dirty clothes now.

The suite's complimentary white, terry cloth robe lay at the foot of the bed where she'd left it that morning.

As quickly as she could, she stripped off her shirt and jeans, stuffed them into a plastic laundry bag from the closet, then slipped into the robe.

Just as she belted it, Myles walked out of the bathroom. "Holland, I…" His gaze moved over her from head-to-toe.

Liquid heat expanding inside of her.

Myles swallowed hard. "You should get into the tub before the water gets cold." He hurried out of the room.

Holland drew in an unsteady breath. As hot as she was feeling right then, there was no danger of that happening.

A moment later, she soaked in the large tub filled with eucalyptus-and-peppermint scented water. A languorous feeling settled over her and she let her mind wander to Myles.

If her bumps and bruises weren't so insistent in reminding her they existed, what she would remember most about today was their first kiss. Which led to another...

Both had been wonderful but way too short. If she wasn't so tired and achy, she might have followed up on those kisses and seen where it led them.

"You can't be seen with a guy ..." Burke's warning crept into Holland's mind, along with the *memory of the attendant at the desk that night, watching her and Myles walk through the lobby.* But what were the chances of the attendant calling a photographer or a reporter?

Still, one photo on social media, that's all it would take to validate Burke's warning... and make the Nash and Gina situation they were trying to fix worse.

A knock echoing on the closed bathroom door broke into her thoughts.

"You okay in there?" Myles called out.

"Yes." Holland replied.

"No dizziness, nausea or a worsening headache?"
Deep concern filled his voice.

"No, none of that." Holland partially sat up in the
tub. "I'll be out in a minute."

"No hurry. Take your time."

He'd asked her that same question on the way
to the hospital and on the drive to the guesthouse.
Every time he'd inquired about her head, it sounded
as if he was reading from a symptom manual for...
head trauma.

Sydney... His wife had hit her head and died in
her sleep.

The realization dropped on Holland almost as
hard as she had tumbled down that hole.

Oh no... What happened to her that evening at
the maze house had probably stirred up so many bad
memories for him.

Was that why he'd insisted on looking after her
tonight? Was he afraid that what happened to Syd-
ney could happen to her?

And here she was worrying about reporters and
tabloids. She should have been concerned about him
like he'd been about her.

After finishing her bath and her nighttime rou-
tine, she put a fresh bandage on her arm and slipped
into her purple sleep shirt.

A short time after she'd crawled in bed, Myles
knocked on the partially opened door.

Holland pulled the beige comforter and sheet a
bit higher. "Come in."

He stepped into the bedroom dressed in black

sweatpants and a T-shirt that fit snuggly to his chest. "I'm just checking on you. Everything okay?"

"I'm good. The bath helped a lot. Thank you."

Holland wanted to ask him if he was okay. But she didn't want to make things harder for him by mentioning Sydney.

"Okay…good." He blew out a breath as he rubbed his hands together. "So, I'll probably be up late watching television in the living room. Just call out if you need anything."

He looked tired. He should be in bed, not hanging out on the couch. But he probably wouldn't listen to her if she told him that. And he probably wasn't planning to sleep in the office either.

Holland glanced at the empty space and extra pillow next to her on the bed.

She looked to him. "There is one thing I would like."

He came farther into the room. The eager to please look on his face was so endearing. "Name it."

"Would you mind holding me while I sleep?"

The request seemed to surprise and please him. "Sure, I just need to turn off the television. Do you want me to set the security alarm?"

She gave him the code and he left to do both.

A short time later, he returned. Mindful of Holland's hurt hip, he got into bed on the other side of her.

She turned off the bedside lamp. In the darkened room, she gravitated toward him and laid her head on his chest.

As she snuggled against him, Myles released a long breath and wrapped an arm around her.

The clean smell of soap emanated from him along with an alluring warmth.

Her eyelids started to droop shut. "Goodnight…"

"Goodnight, Holland." Myles lips ghosted over her forehead.

Whatever his motives were, she was still glad he was there.

Listening to the solid beat of his heart, she relaxed completely and fell asleep.

Chapter Ten

The smell of breakfast nudged Holland awake. As she went to stretch, discomfort made her stop short, and it took a second or two for her to remember why she was so stiff. But she wasn't as sore as she'd been yesterday. The spot on her head was still tender, but her headache was gone. And the best part of waking up feeling better? Myles was still there. Sleeping next to him last night had been better than any kind of pain reliever.

Looking forward to seeing him, she threw back the bedsheets and got up. In the bathroom, she checked out the bruise that ran along the curve of her hip. The doctor had mentioned that, in some fortuitous way, the wooden planks had broken underneath her at the right time, cushioning her fall.

Her phone hadn't been so lucky. It had stopped

working at the hospital. She would contact her assistant later on about sending her a new one.

After taking care of the essentials, she walked out of the bathroom and paused.

Myles was placing a tray with a plate of pancakes and a mug on the bedside table. He glanced over at her. "Good morning."

"Morning."

He was still in his sweatpants and T-shirt. Memories filtered through her mind of resting her cheek on the soft fabric of his shirt and feeling the solid strength of his chest underneath.

The way he'd held her in his arms had felt so perfect. Was it wrong that she wanted to relive that moment again now along with a good-morning kiss? One that would start softly and then deepen into slow, leisurely exploration. A kiss that conveyed the thought "Why rush? We have all day."

As she daydreamed, warmth pooled in Holland's middle, and her breasts grew so heavy it took a little more effort to draw in the breath that she released on a soft sigh.

Myles cleared his throat, blinking as if he were trying to clear a thought. "How's your head?"

Quieting her libido, she focused on alleviating his concerns. "No headache, dizziness or nausea whatsoever."

"Good. I got us pancakes and bacon for breakfast. But if you want something else…"

"No. I love pancakes."

As she walked to the bed, Myles moved out of her

way. "I forgot the syrup. I'll be right back. Do you want anything else?"

Just you. "No. This is perfect. But I could have eaten this in the kitchen. You don't have to spoil me like this."

"Yes, I do. And do you know what you have to do?"

"Pay my taxes and eat chocolate?"

Chuckling, he pointed, indicating she should get under the covers. "Definitely do those things, but that's not it."

When she was propped against the pillows, he handed her the tray. Myles looked into her eyes. "What you need to do is let me take care of you."

Then he bent down and kissed her cheek.

As he walked out, on a reflex, she touched where his lips had been. Warmth and wonderful tingles remained, along with a bit of awe. What he'd just said was almost better than the good-morning kiss she'd dreamed about. When was the last time a guy had said that to her? She couldn't remember one. Not even with Nash. He'd never asked her to let him do anything for her.

In all fairness, Nash wasn't *all* bad. He was really good at grand gestures, like roses, champagne and expensive gifts. But those moments were as scripted as one of his movies. And could only happen after he'd done a two-hour workout, consumed his fourth protein meal of the day, then had a conversation with his agent about a script.

She'd gotten used to doing things for herself.

And it had grown tiring. Not that her schedule

had made doing anything for herself easy. But she'd always wished for something—she'd just never realized it was this. Not a tangible gift, but a simple moment given to her by a guy that was all about her.

But she couldn't get used to Myles taking care of her like this. And she couldn't keep stringing her heart and libido along by claiming she just wanted kisses from him.

Facing that truth took her appetite away.

Myles came back with the syrup. "Here you go. I warmed it up in the microwave. It has butter in it, too, but not a lot.

Regret and frustration pushed out her response. "I can't."

Confusion crossed his face. "You can't have butter? I can warm up some without it."

"No. I can eat butter." But she'd gladly give it up if that would change what she had to tell him. "I can't do this anymore. We have to stop." She set the tray on the nightstand.

He placed the syrup on the tray then sat beside her on the mattress. "I don't understand what you're telling me." Hints of guardedness showed in his puzzled expression. He was anticipating bad news.

"I can't be your friend. I thought I could but it's impossible." His steady gaze, along with the heaviness of disappointment, drove her own gaze to her lap.

Long seconds later he asked. "What do you want us to be?"

Holland looked up, losing herself in his gorgeous

coppery eyes. The confession slipped out. "I want us to be more than *just* friends."

But giving him an honest answer didn't change the facts. She had a fake relationship to maintain, and he had his own baggage from the past.

He looked down a moment then reached for her hand. Without even thinking about it, she turned her palm upward. Myles engulfed her smaller hand with his. "I want to be more than friends with you, too."

A small spark of happiness leaped inside of her then faded away.

It would be so easy to pretend that what he'd just said solved everything. But deep down she knew doing that was just as wrong as most tabloid headlines.

"I love that you feel that way. But there's a problem." Unhappiness about the choices she'd had to make before arriving in Maryland mounted inside her. She released a deep breath. "I don't know if you pay attention to celebrity news. But there's a rumor out there about me spending the night with my ex-boyfriend Nash Moreland while I was visiting the set of his upcoming movie."

Myles's expression remained neutral. "Is it true?"

Did she tell him a shade of the lie and protect Nash, Gina and her production company's interest? That she'd reunited with Nash, but that it was a one and done? Or did she trust Myles and tell him the truth?

She gave his hand a squeeze . "No. It's not. The rumor is part of a whisper campaign to hide the

truth. Nash and his costar Gina Landry slept together. Someone took a picture of them the night
they got together. But it was taken at a bad angle.
You can't tell it's her. Burke, my business partner,
he's handled the photographer and made sure copies
of the photos are gone. But to cloud any speculation
about them being in an intimate relationship, we're
saying it's me."

"So you're doing it to get Nash and his costar out
of a jam?"

"Not just them. She's engaged, and an affair would
tarnish her image. The film they're starring in is the
first major project for my film production company."
Holland sighed. "The bad press could impact the
success of the movie before it's even released. And
the director—it's her first job in that top spot, and
she's fantastic at it. Not to mention all the hard work
the rest of the cast and crew has put into it. None of
them need a rumor about Nash and Gina hanging
over them while they're trying to finish the movie."

Myles looked straight ahead for what felt like an
eternity.

From his profile, she couldn't tell what he was
thinking. "I like you, Myles. That's why I'm telling you this. If I would have known this is where
we were going to end up. I would have been honest
with you sooner."

He looked at her face. Guardedness was no longer
in his. "Do you mind if I get into bed next to you?"

"No." Her heart skittering in her chest, Holland
scooted over to make room for him. As she propped

another pillow against the headboard, Myles got under the covers.

His thigh pressed to hers. The way he wrapped an arm around her, encouraging her to rest her head on his shoulder felt so natural.

He threaded their fingers together on top of the comforter. "Since we're being honest, I haven't wanted to be with anyone in quite a while." He swallowed hard. "I don't want to just end things with you before they've even started. We're only here for a short time. There has to be a way to make it work."

As Holland mulled it over, hopefulness ignited a thought. "Well... Bolan isn't Hollywood. There aren't any photographers potentially hiding in the bushes. And I am researching a documentary about old houses, and you have an interesting old house. Naturally, it makes sense that I would have to consult with you. And that could explain why we're spending a lot of time together."

"Consultations, huh?" He chuckled. "That's an interesting way to explain it."

"But it could work." Her gaze fell to their hands intertwined on the comforter. We would just have to be careful with PDA."

He also looked at their hands.

Not acting like a normal couple in public. That was probably too much to ask.

Wanting to make it easy for him to turn down the idea, she added, "I understand completely if you'd rather not get involved with me."

Myles gaze narrowed in thought as he studied

her face. "When we're by ourselves, can I do this?" He lifted her hand to his lips and gently kissed the back of it.

Nerve endings awakened on her skin. "Yes."

He released her hand. "And what about this?" He leaned in and gave her a lingering kiss.

Desire bloomed inside her. "Definitely a lot of that."

Myles looked into her eyes. "Then we have the answer to our problem."

Not sure she heard him right, Holland leaned away, searching his face for misunderstanding or doubt. "Are you sure?"

"I am." He smiled. "If pretending to be your consultant allows us to be together, I'm all for it."

Holland did have one concern. Her fall had definitely raised memories of Sydney for him. Was he really okay now?

But before she could ask, Myles pressed his mouth back to hers. The kiss was gentle, but it also reflected his steadfast self-assuredness and a rising need that reflected her own.

He prompted her to open to him, and she let him in. His slow, leisurely exploration of the curves and hollows of her mouth, was nothing like their first two kisses. This one was a million times better.

His hand drifted down, and he caressed her breast. The longing for more, to feel him skin to skin uncoiled. They adjusted positions and started scooting downward in anticipation of him lying on top of her.

Her foot tangled in the covers and a twinge went through her hip. She gasped.

Myles rolled to his side. "Did I hurt you?"

"No, I'm just a little sore."

He abruptly got up.

"Wait! Where are you going?"

"I've got calls to make. I'll be in the office."

"But Myles—"

He leaned down and pressed an all-too-quick kiss to her lips. As she tried to pull him back down to her, Myles resisted. A small smile curved up his mouth. "No, we're not doing that. Eat your breakfast."

Later that morning, Myles stacked the clean breakfast dishes on a tray. He didn't have to wash them before setting them outside the door, but he appreciated the distraction.

After a long cold shower that he'd really needed, and making phone calls to contractors, he'd gone back to the bedroom to check on Holland.

She'd finished breakfast and had fallen asleep. He'd been tempted to kiss her, but that would only lead to him needing another cold shower. It had only been just yesterday that she'd been injured— he should have been in better control.

But just like he'd predicted, once he'd gotten a taste of her, he'd been lost.

He was going to have to learn to control himself if was going to pretend he was just acting as a consultant for her documentary.

A memory from years ago, elusive, and quick,

started to emerge, casting a shadow of doubt that he'd made the right choice to be with Holland.

Myles barred it from his thoughts. His past didn't factor into this.

But what about him being here with her now? When they'd walked through the lobby, no one had paid attention. Although the clerk behind the front desk had been staring. But considering the shape Holland was in, that was understandable. But now that he and Holland were planning to spend more time together, should he leave the guesthouse? It would definitely make it easier for him to keep his hands to himself until her bruises faded.

As Myles set the dishes outside the door in the hallway, he couldn't stop himself from peering to the end of the vacant hallway.

Now he was getting paranoid.

He went to the office. The clothes he'd slept in were lying on the couch and he stashed them in his duffel.

As he picked up his phone from the side table, his gaze wandered to the desk, where his laptop was next to hers. The letter and fabric they'd found was also there in a clear plastic sleeve.

Holland had been so disappointed about not being able to find records about the house. Luckily, as he'd mentioned, he had all of his records of ownership. His attorney was thorough when it came to paper.

An idea came to mind, and Myles sat down on the couch, scrolling through numbers on his phone until he found the one for his attorney, Rick Fischer. The last time he'd talked to Rick was when the attorney had walked him through the documents for Sydney's estate. It had all been a blur. But he'd already known what to expect as to her last wishes.

Shortly after they'd gotten married, Myles had been the one to insist they draw up their wills and the necessary powers of attorney and compile documents with information that might be needed. He'd always envisioned him not being there and Sydney being the one who had to sort through everything. Not him.

A small hint of the remembered numbness and disbelief he'd experienced back then, crept in now. Along with the confusion he'd felt when the attorney had mentioned the house. Sydney had used an inheritance she'd received from her grandmother to buy it. He'd insisted she keep that money for herself, separated from their joint accounts. That's why he'd never known about it. And the timing of the purchase—it had been when they were going through marriage counseling. Why buy him a house? He still didn't know the answer, but like Dante had said, maybe there wasn't one.

Pushing questions aside, he dialed the Rick's number. He was put on hold. A short time later, the older man picked up and they exchanged greetings.

"What can I do for you?" Rick asked.

"You helped my wife, Sydney, purchase a house in Bolan, Maryland, before she died. I'm just getting around to looking at it. I'm interested in the property history records. If I have them, I can't access them right now, and the town is having computer system issues. They also can't locate the physical records."

The man chuckled wryly. "I'm not surprised. I remember working with the people in Bolan. It was an interesting experience. The real estate attorney down there is the one who actually drew up the documents. But we should have something in our files. Or at least I can put you in touch with the attorney who did the search. Is there a problem with the house from a legal perspective?"

"No." Feeling the need to stand, Myles rose from the couch. He spoke the thought now at the forefront of his mind. "Knowing the history of the house might give me some insight into why my wife bought it."

"Ah, yes." The man sighed. "I can't help you find closure with that, but I can help you hunt down the records you're interested in."

After confirming how to reach Myles, they ended the call.

Closure. Why did everyone automatically make that leap?

But he hadn't told the attorney about the letter, so of course he'd think that.

Myles went to the desk. A hint of the doubt he'd felt earlier, tried to weave into his thoughts. No. He'd reached closure on everything he'd needed to when it came to him and Sydney. His focus now was helping Holland find out the origin of the letter. That's all.

Chapter Eleven

Holland sat on the couch in the suite, watching a British crime drama on the flat-screen television. But her mind kept wandering to Myles's text message on her new phone.

He was working on the plumbing at the house with Scott and wouldn't come back to the suite until later that night. He'd reminded her to eat dinner.

After revealing everything to him day before yesterday and agreeing they both wanted to spend more time together, she'd envisioned their relationship progressing a little faster. But he was keeping his distance.

If only she hadn't gotten her foot twisted in the covers the other morning. The awkward position had strained her hip a little, that's all. She wasn't in a huge amount of pain. They could have continued what they were doing. She'd *wanted* it to continue, even though she'd fallen asleep. She'd actually dreamed of them being together. It was all she could think about.

But now Myles would barely go past a kiss. The most provocative thing he'd done was touch her butt during a kiss in the kitchen that morning. And then it was like they were playing the hot potato game and her backside was the first thing he needed to let go of as quickly as possible.

Her phone rang on the couch beside her. *Myles*.

She picked up, unable to stop the smile on her face. "Hello."

"Hi. Did you see my text message?"

"Yes."

"Did you eat?"

Yes, Dad... Holland held back the remark. Myles spoiling her with attention had been fun at first, but now he was sounding more like a parent. She already had parents. What she also had were unfulfilled needs that required him to be naked...and here with her, not miles away at his house.

Holland let her head drop on the back of the couch. "Yes. I've eaten."

"Good. Hey, I might not make it there tonight."

"Why not?" The slight wail of discontent in her voice made her inwardly wince. Sounding like a child wouldn't help her cause.

"Scott and I just got back from making a run to the store, and we're just starting to work on the kitchen sink. I don't want to wake you up. You need your rest."

"I'm rested." Holland nearly gritted her teeth.

"Well, keep resting. I want you to take it easy. Oh, I received the property records from my attorney."

Myles had mentioned reaching out to him. The hope of good news made her sit up straight. "And?"

"And they're not helpful. None of the past owners' first or last names begin with an *L* or *B*. I'm sorry."

"It was worth a shot. I appreciate you trying." But as much as she wanted answers to the letter, she'd trade that for time with him. "I miss you."

Seconds fell into a long pause. "I miss you, too. I better go. Scott's waiting for me."

They said their goodbyes.

For a long moment, Holland stared at her phone. He'd hesitated in saying he missed her. Had something changed? Maybe he wasn't that anxious to see her. And perhaps it had nothing to do with his concern over her bruises.

Maybe he was still dealing with trauma from her accident reminding him of what happened to Sydney. She'd never gotten around to asking him. Had contacting his attorney also been a reminder? Was that why he was pulling away?

No longer interested in the show on television, Holland went to bed. Unable to sleep, she sent a text to Chloe.

I'm frustrated.

Oh no, are you still hurting? I hope you're resting

Unfortunately, yes.

I know—frustrating not to be running around doing research, but you should take it easy.

Not understanding what was happening with Myles, and remembering what he'd said earlier in their conversation about her taking it easy, pushed her over the edge.

I am fine! My head is fine! My hip is fine! How many times do I have to tell you?

Dots floated in a text bubble.

Once? I just asked you now.

Ugh! Now she was yelling in a text at her friend for no reason.

I'm sorry. It's not you. It's Myles. All he wants to do is feed me, make sure I rest and hold me.

Chloe responded with a series of question marks and exclamation points, then…

Um… I think your response to that is supposed to be thank you, more please.

Holland sighed. Did she dare put it into words? He'd said he didn't want to just end things with her before they'd even started. That he'd wanted to try and make things work so they could have a relationship. But maybe he wasn't ready.

I'm being ungrateful, but I really like Myles. I thought we were heading into something, but now I'm not sure he feels the same way.

Seconds ticked by as once again dots floated in a text bubble.

He was really worried about you. He's there. He cares!

But he wasn't there. Maybe he just didn't know how to tell her why he wasn't. And trying to explain how she felt about that to Chloe was difficult, and she didn't feel like doing it in a text.

You're right. I'm just tired.

Love you. Get some rest. I'll check on you in the morning

Rest? How could she rest knowing that she and Myles might face a ~~tough~~ about him changing his mind? *THOUGHT*

Holland finally fell asleep, but a few hours later she woke up restless. And maybe a little hungry. As she thought of the salted caramel candied bacon ice cream in the freezer, her mouth watered. She could use a snack and eating ice cream always lifted her mood.

She got up. In the hallway, moonlight streamed through small openings in the blinds, illuminating the way through the living room.

In the kitchen, she turned on the lights, then found a bowl and teaspoon. She took the ice cream from the freezer and opened it on the counter.

It was too solid for a teaspoon, so she reached for the large metal serving spoon in the drawer. If she ran it under warm water, it would cut through the ice cream.

Holland retrieved the spoon and took it to the faucet. It took a minute for the water to heat up, but if that was the only sacrifice she had to make in waiting to eat ice cream, it was worth it.

"You okay?"

Startled, Holland let out a squeak, turned and threw the spoon a split second before she registered Myles's presence.

As the spoon came at him, Myles quickly leaned to the left, and it sailed past his head.

She should have been concerned about almost hitting him. But his bare abs rippling above his low-slung sweats and the natural V cutting along his hips held her attention. His solid chest was just as extraordinary. He'd obviously been sleeping in the office, but his heavy-lidded eyes, thrown in with the rest of all that goodness, only made him the epitome of just-woke-up sexy.

Holland grew overly warm and a little light-headed. She needed to stop ogling him but… "This is torture—"

"What's wrong?" Concern filled Myles's tone as he strode over to her, but his voice, husky from just waking up, enhanced the rest of him…in a terribly wonderful way.

"Where are you hurting?" He searched her face. "Is it your head or your hip?"

"No. I'm…" Holland was at a loss for words. It wasn't either of those places. She was hot and bothered, and *he* was the cause.

"I'll take you to bed."

If only he would…

As Myles went to scoop her up in his arms, she batted his hands away. "No, this isn't fair."

"What are you talking about? What's not fair?"

Holland couldn't hold back any longer. It all came rushing out. "Me falling though a porch and getting hurt. You being here. That stupid little string holding up your pants that practically screams 'untie me to find out if what's under there matches all of this." She circled her hand in the air, encompassing him. "And if you think I'm saying any of this because I hit my head, that's not it."

Myles staring at her with a bewildered look on his face made Holland want to climb into one of the bottom cabinets with her spoon and tub of ice cream. But she'd gone this far—she might as well finish.

She took a breath and a beat to slow down. "I know you're second guessing us getting involved. And that's okay. Be honest with me. That way, we both know where we stand."

Myles brow raised. "Are you done?"

"Yes."

"Good." He stopped mere inches in front of her.

Don't ogle his chest. Holland looked down. Nope, not helping.

Myles tipped up her chin and made her look at his face. "You might think you know where I stand when it comes to you. But you're not even close."

The intense longing and raw hunger flashing in his eyes made her take in a quick breath.

Myles captured her mouth with his, and surprise morphed into longing. He caressed down her shoulders and grasped her waist. Holland laid her palms on his chest, and the heat of his skin ignited a slow flame, fueled by growing desire. She opened to him, matching him stroke for stroke in a tantalizing exploration. Seeking...finding...wanting so much more.

As she glided her hands to his shoulders, he swept kisses across her cheek and down her throat. Her nipples tingled—the friction from her shirt as they grazed over his hard chest was sensual torture. But she wasn't alone. Myles caressed down her back. Holding on to her curves, he pressed them closer together, and she felt the urgency of his need.

He stopped kissing her and moved a fraction

away. The loss of heat and pleasure combined with the natural coolness of the room made her shiver.

Tension emanated from him, and his hands flexed on her hips. "Holland—" The huskiness of his tone made her shiver again. "We should stop."

Stop? Was he insane! "No," she moaned softly.

Myles caught her hands with his and pressed them to his chest.

As he looked into her eyes, the intensity of need burned bright, but so did frustration. "It's not that I don't want to. When I changed my mind about coming here tonight, I just tossed a change of clothes in my bag. But, I—I don't have anything."

It took a second for what he'd just said to click in her mind. Did he mean protection? Relief sent an exhale out of her along with a quiet laugh. "That's not a problem at all. I have condoms."

A breath rushed out of him. "Thank you."

His words were so reverent, she wondered if he wasn't thanking her but offering up a prayer.

But Myles picking her up and carrying to the bedroom erased all worry about what was next.

As soon as he set her down next to the bed, need fueled every kiss and caress. Every hurried tug and glide to take their clothing off so they could fall together on the bed.

Finally, Holland felt the warmth of him, skin to skin.

Sighs purred from her as his lips swept down her throat to breast. He sucked her nipple into his mouth, then traced around it with his tongue. Desire spiraled deep inside her as her world shrank to the molten warmth of his mouth. As if sensing her pleasure, he moved to her other breast and did the same.

As he kissed and caressed her body, he paid attention, repeating what made her arch up. Hold on to him tighter. Call out his name in ecstasy as he slid his hand between her thighs and took her over the edge.

She wanted to explore him, too. After he retrieved a condom and came back to her, she started to tell him.

But Myles gliding himself inside her stole the rest of her words. He whispered in her ear, "Next time."

They found their rhythm, moving in sync. He took her higher and higher, and she lost herself in the onslaught of erotic sensation. She hovered in the space of wanting to orgasm and not wanting to free fall into overwhelming pleasure.

Myles lifted her hips higher, seating himself impossibly deeper with every sure stroke.

A moment later, her climax hit, and his quickly followed.

It felt as if there was no end. No beginning between them. They were one.

Afterwards, as they held each other, she stroked her hand over his chest, reveling in their new intimacy.

"What changed your mind about coming here tonight?" She asked.

"Isn't it obvious why I'm here?" He caressed up

and down her back, leaving a trail of alluring warmth. "I missed you."

Hearing him say that made her so happy. "You should have woken me up."

"True." Myles chuckled. "I got off lucky. You're pretty lethal with a cooking spoon."

Playfully, she poked him. "And don't you forget it."

"Trust me. I won't." He held her closer. "I wanted to wake you up when I came in, but you looked so peaceful. And honestly, I didn't trust myself. You have no idea how hard it's been to keep my hands off of you."

She leaned away to look at him. "So why did you?"

"You were just hurt the other day." He lightly traced near the scratches on her arm. "I didn't want to be selfish. I wanted you to be able to enjoy the moment. I wanted it to feel right for both of us."

The way he took care of her and put her first—she could easily get used to that. "Well it was perfect."

"Perfect, huh?" A sexy smile took over his mouth "I think I can do better than that."

"Really?" As Holland tried to imagine what better might look like, she shivered in anticipation. "What are you going for?"

As Myles rolled her on her back, he massaged her breast. His thumb feathering over her nipple, spiraled desire down to her core. As he kissed her, he murmured, "Unforgettable."

He made good on his word.

As Holland swam in pure pleasure, a fleeting thought invaded her mind—she wished they had more time.

Chapter Twelve

The next morning, as Holland carried two mugs into the bedroom, a cloud of steam floated from the spa bathroom.

Myles was in the shower? Anticipation made her speed up. She'd thought they were enjoying coffee in bed. Like she cared he'd changed the plan. She wasn't going to miss *that* view.

As visions of being with him last night flashed in her mind, her skin tingled. They'd definitely reached a milestone in their new relationship. New *secret* relationship. A part of her bristled at the word *secret*. They weren't hiding. They were just being discreet by not announcing it to the world.

In the bathroom, she put the mugs on the counter. Hot coffee sloshed over her fingers, but she didn't feel it.

Awestruck, she stared at him in the corner shower as the water rained down on him from above. It was hotter than the coffee that had just splashed on her fingers.

Just as she went to whip her sleep shirt over her head, the buzzer sounded from the door.

Myles paused in soaping up. "Did you order room service?"

"No, it's probably Chloe." Holland inwardly groaned. "Last night, she told me she was going to stop by. I forgot. I better answer it. Otherwise, she might think something is wrong."

He started rinsing off. "Can you stall her until I get out of here?"

The be-careful-with-PDA rule didn't apply when it came to Chloe.

If anyone understood discretion, she did.

"Finish your shower and come out when you're ready."

"Are you sure?" Myles looked surprised.

"I am." She leaned partway into the stall, and he met her halfway for a kiss.

The steam rising around them, and the warmth of his mouth was like an aphrodisiac, pulling her in.

Holland reluctantly took her lips from his. "I have to go."

The smile tipping up his mouth shifted to a frown. "I need a shirt."

Chloe rang the buzzer several times.

Holland pointed to the bedroom. "I've got a shirt you can wear. It's a men's large." Interpreting the "hell no" look on his face, she added, "It's not an ex-boyfriend's shirt—it's mine. I'll leave it on the bed."

She retrieved the garment from the dresser drawer and tossed it near the headboard.

Debating between wiping away the image of him in the shower, or keeping it center stage in her mind, she snagged her cardigan from the side chair by the bed.

Knocks echoed from the front of the suite as she closed the bedroom door behind her.

"*Coming!*" she called out. Pulling on the sweater, she hurried to the entryway. Remembering to turn off the alarm, she keyed in the code, then opened the door.

She smiled at Chloe. "Hi."

"Good morning." Her friend quickly walked in and hugged her. "I was just about to call you. Did I wake you?"

"No. I've been up for a while."

As Holland shut the door, Chloe set her purse on the coffee table and sat down. "Is Myles here?"

"He's in the shower."

Chloe glanced from the guestroom bathroom to the closed bedroom door, then back to Holland. "So you and Myles are…?"

Holland couldn't stop a smile as she dropped down next to Chloe on the couch. "It just happened. Everything I texted you last night about what I thought he felt—I was so wrong."

"Oh crap…" Chloe's expression turned grim. "This is worse than I thought."

Holland's happiness diminished. Her best friend had never been so unsupportive. "What's wrong with Me and Myles getting together?"

"Nothing but...have you spoken to Burke or any of your people today?"

"No. I turned my phone off last night after I texted you. Why? What's happened?"

"The best thing is for me to show you." Chloe removed her phone from her purse, flipped through items on the screen, then handed it to Holland.

An online celebrity news page was visible, and Holland read the featured headline.

Nash Moreland's Return: He's exploring new movie roles and engaging with the past in life and love.

He wouldn't. He didn't...

Holland glanced farther down the page, and her stomach plummeted. She felt the same way as Chloe. This was worse than she thought, too.

The bedroom door opened, and Myles walked out, wearing the T-shirt she'd left for him.

She recalled the story behind it. She'd been filming scenes for a movie at a flea market. In between takes, a nervous intern had spilled an entire thirty-two-ounce cup of cherry lemonade on her. Rather than lose momentum with the scene, she'd grabbed the shirt from a nearby stall, made sure the vendor got paid and got back to filming.

The dancing dolphins in the graphic on the front

of it looked even happier stretched across Myles's hard chest.

As he headed toward the guest room, he smiled at Chloe. "Good morning."

"Same to you." Chloe gave him a cheery smile that disappeared as soon as he shut the door behind him. Worry filled her face as she lowered her voice. "What are you going to do about Nash, and what are you going to tell Myles?"

"Burke is going to have to handle Nash. And Myles…" Holland glanced at the closed door. They'd just gotten together. How would he take this new development? "I don't know what to tell him. We just worked through the fake relationship stuff with Nash. But this…" She pointed to the news page on Chloe's phone. "It might scare him off."

Chloe laid her hand on Holland's arm. "I know you're worried, but can I give you some advice?"

"Always."

"You have to tell him everything and be prepared for the worst. You view the situation with Nash as just pretend, but Myles might not be able to see it that way. If that's the case, ending things with him now would save you both a lot of heartache. I know that's not what you want to hear. But you know as well as I do that the industry we work in can be hard on personal relationships. Even short-term ones."

"You're right." Frustration and anxiety made Holland drop her head into her hands. "But Myles and I just figured out how to be together. This isn't fair."

Chloe patted her back. "Is there anything I can do?"

"No." As Holland lifted her head, she couldn't keep the glumness out of her voice. "You've given me good advice. I appreciate it. Well actually, there is one thing you could do. You could fly to California and put a muzzle on Nash."

Irritation on Holland's behalf flickered in Chloe's eyes. "Trust me, I wish I could. Nash is a liability to himself and everyone else involved in the situation. Tell Burke that he and Nash's people need to get him under control, and fast." She stood. "I have a meeting with an interviewer, but I'm free later. Call me if you need me."

They hugged goodbye and after Chloe left.

Holland spent the next ten minutes reading and listening to urgent voicemails from Burke, her publicist, and some new person who'd been brought in by Nash's publicist for damage control.

The gist of all their messages? All they wanted her to do was smile happily for any photographers, say, "No comment.", if anyone asked her about Nash. And the new person had echoed what Burke had told her before. She shouldn't risk being seen with anyone in public who might raise speculation about her and Nash's relationship.

Myles walked out of the room carrying his packed duffel bag and looking all kinds of wonderful in a long-sleeved blue pullover, jeans and boots. He glanced around. "Chloe left already?"

"Yes. She could only stop by for a few minutes."

He went to the kitchen and set up the Keurig. "Do you want coffee?"

"No, thank you."

"Sorry, I don't have time to eat breakfast with you. They're working on the siding today. I need to be at the house to meet them."

"That's okay. I'm not really hungry." Just the idea of adding caffeine to the nerves swirling around her stomach made Holland feel ill. And so did waiting to tell him what was going on. "I know you need to leave, but do you have a minute to talk?"

Myles paused from taking a teaspoon from a drawer and looked at her. "Sure."

Trying to lessen his concern, Holland forced a smile. "I can wait until after you make your coffee."

But Myles was concerned. It was evident in his slightly drawn brows and in his deliberate movements, from taking the full cup from the machine to stirring sugar into his coffee.

As he walked out of the kitchen, she took a seat on the couch. But instead of joining her, he sat on one of the stools at the counter and faced her.

Holland pointed. "Don't you want to sit next to me?"

"I do. And I also want to kiss you. But I want to stay focused on what you have to say." He took a sip of coffee.

Kisses might never be on the agenda with Myles again once she told him what was happening.

Holland took a deep breath. "So, do you remember the situation I told you about the two costars in a film my company is producing?"

"Nash and Gina. I do. They're the reason why a

story is being floated around about you spending the night with him." A wry smile ghosted over his lips. "They're also why I'm a consultant helping you with research on your new documentary."

"Right." He'd definitely paid attention. "Well, there's been a small development. Last night, Nash was live on a late-night show. A few cocktails were served. The host started asking him about Gina, and…"

"And what?"

"First Nash said a few things that made it sound like he had a thing for Gina. When the host sprang the news that he'd heard a rumor about him and Gina fooling around, Nash panicked and went off script."

Myles set his mug on the counter. Although he remained calm, wariness was in his eyes. "How far off?"

Reading what Nash had said was one thing. Saying it out loud was another. Especially to Myles. She'd hoped for repeats of last night. This could ruin that opportunity, and honestly, she wouldn't blame him if he decided to steer clear of her.

Holland closed her eyes a moment. "He said that we had more than just a one-night hookup. That we were officially back together. And he hinted that we're planning to get engaged."

"Is there an engagement in your future?"

"No, of course not!" Holland quickly crossed the room and stood in front of him. "This is just as false as what was put out with the whisper campaign."

He took her hand. "So how does it work? Your publicists deny it? You say 'no comment'?"

Neither confirm nor deny. That's what her publicist and Nash's had basically said was the plan. "If we say there's no engagement, people might automatically focus on the Gina rumor. And it makes Nash look bad. Like he drank too much, then said too much."

"Isn't that what happened?"

"Yes. But we need him to look good."

Myles released a long breath. "I won't pretend that I understand how Hollywood and celebrity images work. Honestly, the only thing I care about is spending time with you while we're together."

"We will, but..." Now the hard part. "The two of us spending a lot of time together because you're my consultant probably isn't a good idea. The person handling damage control for Nash said I shouldn't risk being seen with anyone who might raise speculation about me and Nash."

He released a harsh chuckle. Frustration shadowed his eyes as he released her hand and picked up his mug. After a long sip, he met her gaze. "So because Nash screwed up your fake relationship, we have to put even more limits on our real one."

"Yes, but it's temporary."

"How long is that? Tomorrow? A few days? Next week?"

At least a week after the filming ended on Nash and Gina's movie. Longer than she or Myles planned to remain in town.

He huffed a breath. "Got it. Not anytime soon."

Before she could answer, Myles's phone rang on the counter, and he glanced at the screen. "It's the siding repair company." He answered the call. "Hello. Yes…yes. No, not a problem. I'll be there. Thank you." He hung up. "The contractor is running early."

"I understand."

"Do you?" Myles set his mug and phone aside. "Since I've known you, you've been in a pretend relationship, and now a pretend engagement. I don't want to be in a pretend anything. I just want to be with you." He shook his head and stood. "I have to go."

He planted a long, lingering kiss on her mouth. It tasted of coffee and sweetness… and a hint of doubt.

After Myles left, she straightened the kitchen and the living room. After beating the throw pillows on the couch into submission, she stood near the kitchen counter feeling alone and at loose ends. Right then, she just wished she could roll back time to earlier that morning, when things were good between her and Myles. Or better yet, she wished she could travel back in time and shut Nash up.

"I just want to be with you…"

Remembering what Myles had said made her happy and sad at the same time. She wanted that, too. To give them both a shot at having something *real for as long as they could.* But she had to protect the investment in the film, and outside of Gina and Nash, she needed to look after the rest of the cast and crew who relied upon and trusted her.

Like Chloe had warned her, maybe Myles couldn't

take the new constraints on their barely three-day old relationship. But could she really blame him for being wary? Especially after everything he'd been through. The last thing she wanted was for him to get hurt.

A text buzzed in on her phone. Her pulse leaped in her throat. Was it Myles? She took her phone from her pocket. No. It was Chloe.

Did you tell him?

Yes.

And?

Holland glimpsed Myles's duffel bag under the counter. He'd forgotten it. Probably because he'd been frustrated over what she'd told him. Holland responded to Chloe's question with the truth.

I don't know.

Chapter Thirteen

Myles stood out back assessing the work being done on the clapboard siding.

The outside of the house had been carefully power washed with a bleach solution last week to counteract the light mold and mildew he'd found in some areas. Today they were sanding it down to the wood and replacing any boards that were damaged. The next step was painting the outside of the house.

While the contractors were handling the outside, he should get started on the kitchen cabinets. Or he could call Holland. And say what? He'd probably said too much already.

Their relationship was only a few days old. Did he really have a say in anything she chose to do? The whole whisper campaign she'd mentioned with her and Nash... No, he didn't like it. But it was just a rumor. Still, Nash claiming they had a relationship and Holland going along with it was a whole other level of secrets. It had *consequences*.

Should he have been more cautious about diving in too fast with Chloe? It was starting to feel like not waiting like he usually did to assess the entire situation was a mistake.

His mind started to peel back layers of the past, revealing what he'd worked hard to reconcile and put away.

His phone rang. From the distinctive chime, Myles already knew the caller. It was Dante.

He answered. "Hey, Dante, what's up?"

"I'm good." From the faraway sound of his brother's voice, Dante had him on speakerphone. "What's up with you? I called you earlier this morning."

After he'd left Tillbridge, Myles had spotted that his brother had called. But with so much weighing on his mind about his talk with Holland, he'd planned on calling him later.

"I was caught up with some things." Myles leaned on the wood covered by the tarp. "But I was going to call you later."

"By things you mean Holland?"

The other day, when he and Dante had briefly talked, he'd told Dante about what Holland and what happened to her at the maze house.

"Yes." *Definitely Holland.*

"How is she? I'm guessing she's still pretty bruised up after that fall."

The vision of them being together last night flashed

in mind. He heart kicked up a beath and he cleared his throat. "She's good."

"What happened and why are you stressed about it?"

"What happened? What do you mean?"

Dante chuckled. "You must have forgotten who you're talking to right now. You sound off, and you just answered a question with question. Something's up."

He could deny it. But he didn't want to. "Me and Holland...we slept together last night."

"Okay, then, she is doing better. So is this the start of something or a onetime thing?"

"I'm not sure. She has some issues going on with her ex."

"What kind of issues?"

Ones that were hella complicated to explain. Myles rubbed the back of his neck. Maybe he shouldn't have gone down this road of conversation. "Forget it. It doesn't matter."

"It does, otherwise you wouldn't have mentioned it."

His brother had a point. The need to unburden himself prompted Myles to speak. "Take me off speaker."

"Okay, you're off."

Myles weighed what he could say. He probably shouldn't mention names. "There was an issue with two of the actors connected to one of Holland's films. I can't go into details, but to protect the film and the people involved, she's pretending to be engaged to someone."

"Oh… I see. And it's reminding you of the past?"

Myles released a slightly bitter chuckle. "In the worst way possible." If he and Sydney hadn't…

Dante's request to change to a video call dinged in. Myles accepted it, and a slimmer, younger version of his own face appeared on screen.

From the background, he could tell Dante was sitting at his desk. "Do you want to be with Holland?"

"Yes, I do. At least for the time we have left."

Dante looked away a moment. "I know what I'm about to say is going to sound wrong to you, but hear me out. You haven't wanted to be with anyone since Sydney. That's huge in my book. And from how you've described her, Holland is just the person you need right now. And with you knowing something about the situation she's in, have you considered that you might be good for her, too?"

But it wasn't the same or was it? Myles released a long, steady breath. "No, I hadn't considered that."

"I also think it will give you a needed perspective on a few things."

"You mean closure."

"I didn't say that. *You* did. What I am saying is, instead of overthinking the past or even the future, maybe you should ask yourself an important question—does the enjoyment of being with Holland for the short term outweigh everything else?"

Later that morning, as Myles painted window trim, his conversation with Dante reverberated in his mind. Could it be that in some weird way, being in this situation was good for him and Holland?

The sound of a car engine echoed. He set down the brush and opened the front door.

Holland got out of her parked car, carrying his duffel bag.

So much had been on his mind, he hadn't realized he'd left it at the suite.

Dressed similar to him, in her own signature way, she looked strong and healthy. He was glad about that. And he couldn't deny he was also glad to see her.

As she climbed the porch steps, Holland gave him a tentative smile. "You left your bag. I thought you might want it."

"Thanks." He accepted it. "Do you want to come in?"

She nodded. "Yes, but just for minute. I know you're busy."

He set his duffel bag down near the wall.

Holland tucked her hands in her back pockets and looked down to where she toed a raised nail in the floor with her boot. "I also came by to apologize. It wasn't okay for me to assume that you would be on-board with hiding anything. The situation I'm in is a lot. And I don't expect you to want to be a part of it."

As Holland turned to walk away, the sun hit her face, and the memory of when he'd first met her and thought she was trespassing came to mind. Because of his limited assumptions about her, he'd sent her away. But he'd gotten a second chance to see her again, know her, be with her. She made him laugh. She surprised him and made him embrace spontaneity. Around her, he'd started to just feel something again. Did that last part scare him? Yes. But in answer to Dante's question, all of that did outweigh everything else.

Myles caught her by the hand. "Holland, wait. Don't go yet."

He wasn't ready for either of them to walk away from what they'd barely started. But if he wanted to continue things with Holland and have peace of mind, he had to tell her more about his past.

Holland let Myles tug her back to him. He grasped hold of her waist, brought her closer and pressed his mouth to hers.

Hope and desire ramped up her heart rate as she leaned against him. The scent of her body wash mixed appealingly with his own woodsy scent, warmed by body heat.

But instead of deepening the kiss, Myles ended it and took a step back. "I need to tell you something. Can we go for a walk?"

"Sure."

Hand in hand, they crossed the backyard to the makeshift road behind the trees.

As they walked, Myles looked so serious. A ball of nerves rolled around inside her during the silence between them.

He finally spoke. "I can see why you're extending yourself to fix the situation with Nash. It's about business, and anyone who's ever been responsible for something has had to make sacrifices, including holding information back."

"But you don't approve of how we're constructing a lie."

"No. I can't say that. Because if I did, I would be a hypocrite."

Unease made Holland pause. Oh no…had his wife cheated on him? Or maybe he was the one who'd had an affair.

Myles faced her. "The last ten months of my marriage to Sydney weren't real."

"So you weren't married?"

"We were, but in name only."

Shock stalled Holland's steps. She had so many questions, but she kept silent, waiting for him to fill in the blanks. Walking with him, she synced with his slow pace.

"We had a good four years together," he said. "I used to think couples who claimed they'd drifted apart were just making up a weak excuse for why their marriage hadn't worked. But that's exactly what happened with me and Sydney. We tried to salvage our relationship and did all we could do to reignite the spark. We even went to marriage counseling before throwing in the towel. It took the equivalent of a slap in the face for us to finally wake up to it."

"What happened?"

"I went home for lunch one afternoon to grab a change of clothes. I'd planned on meeting some of the guys I worked with at a sports bar in town that night after work. I walked in on Sydney's mother and sister setting up gifts on the dining room table. They'd hung a banner on the wall that said, Happy Fifth Anniversary."

"Oh no...you'd forgotten?"

"Yep. They were leaving a surprise for me and Sydney to find when we came home from work. Her mom and sister had even put a cake and champagne in the refrigerator. They made me promise to not spoil it for Sydney. When she came home and saw everything, I could tell by her face that she'd forgotten, too."

Holland tried to imagine what he and his late wife must have felt. Loss? Regret? "That must have been a tough wake-up call to face."

"Yes, but we had the longest, most honest conversation than we'd had in a long time. We knew it was over between us, but with her family's view on marriage and divorce, we were facing an uphill battle, especially Sydney. If we wanted an amicable, drama-free divorce, we couldn't tell them, or our friends, until after we'd split. She also wanted to wait until after her sister's wedding that fall and the winter holidays. Her family always had big celebrations for Thanksgiving and Christmas."

"So you two pretended to be married for ten whole months?" Holland couldn't keep the incredulousness out of her voice. She had trouble agreeing to be Nash's pretend girlfriend and fiancée for a short time, but a faking an *entire marriage*?

Myles shrugged. "Honestly, it was an extension of what we were already doing. We just slept in separate rooms and didn't have to be accountable to each other. The only thing we had to do was be a couple around our family and friends."

"But it couldn't have been that easy?"

Myles stared ahead, his expression far away, as if he was seeing the past instead of the trees and dirt road in front of him. "Lying to her family and our friends…no. But the trade-off was the level of honesty *we* had with each other about our relationship. I guess that's what made it easy for Sydney to move on."

Holland hesitated to speculate on what he wasn't saying. "Move on as in find someone else?"

Myles nodded. "His name was Jake. He lived in Santa Barbara."

"Didn't that complicate things?"

"It did. She felt torn between wanting to be with him and continuing to keep up appearances. I suggested we tell her family, but…" Myles stopped walking, and they faced each other. As he stared past Holland, he seemed to grapple for the words. "The last weeks before her sister's wedding was supposed to take place, she faced a lot of pressure. By then, I'd quit my job in construction in Pennsylvania and was working in New York full-time with my brother. But we told everyone my relocation was temporary. That

I was just helping my brother with a project. She was traveling a lot with her job and spending long weekends in Santa Barbara with Jake. Her family started to notice how much we were apart. The suggestion was made that she should quit her job in support of me and our marriage."

Antiquated thinking like that set Holland's teeth on edge. "I bet she hated hearing that."

Myles met her gaze. "She really did." He looked down as he took Holland's other hand in his. "That day before her sister found her, her parents had really gone after her about devoting more time to our marriage and starting a family. It upset her. That's why she went home instead of spending the night at her parents'. And ended up dying alone."

Tears pricked her eyes. "I'm so sorry, Myles."

She couldn't imagine the pain and grief he must have felt in the aftermath of Sydney's death. As he gripped Holland's hands a bit tighter, she squeezed back, letting him know she was there, willing to just stand there with him as the breeze blew and the limbs of the trees swayed above them.

He continued. "Sydney's suitcase and carry-on were by the front door. Whenever she traveled, she always printed her itinerary and boarding pass, just in case, and stuck it in the side pocket of her carry-on. She was heading to California in the morning. Her family assumed she was coming to me and following up on their advice about our marriage."

Myles looked up, and Holland met his gaze and

her own assumptions. She'd thought the sorrow that showed up in his eyes when he'd spoken of Sydney was just for the loss of her as his wife. But now she understood it went far beyond that. He also hurt for the opportunity that Sydney had missed—a chance to move on with her life, and possible happiness with Jake. And, she imagined, also crushing guilt for not letting go sooner.

The rest of the truth hit Holland, and her heart ached even more for him. "You never told her family."

He shook his head. "It was Sydney's story to tell, not mine. Maybe she would have after her sister got married. I did call Jake. I was going to work out a way for him to say goodbye to her. But he was too broken up to talk. He hung up, and I never heard from him again."

"I'm so sorry that happened to you." Holland wrapped her arms around him. Myles kissed her temple. "And I'm also sorry for what Sydney lost."

Myles leaned away and looked at Holland's face. "Remembering what happened to her made me realize something. I know we just met, but I enjoy being with you. I don't want to lose out on spending time with you, even if that means we can't let anyone else know."

"Are you sure? Because I feel the same way."

"I'm sure." Myles tightened his embrace, and Holland met him for kiss that she felt all the way down to her toes.

Her and Myles being together—this could work.

He wasn't immersed in the glitzy Hollywood world, but he understood the task she faced. And she understood his initial concerns.

Now she just had to control the variables of the situation with her and Nash and not let them get in the way...

Chapter Fourteen

A few days later, Holland stood shoulder to shoulder with Myles in the kitchen at Chloe and Tristan's house. She sliced a tomato into quarters, then put it in the metal bowl next to the clear cutting board.

He handed her another tomato from the half dozen on the counter in front of him.

She smiled. "Thank you."

He grinned back. "You're welcome."

"Seriously?" Chloe carried a platter of seasoned chicken ready for the grill. "It takes two of you to make a garden salad? If dinner was up to you guys, we'd starve. Hurry up already." She gave them a playfully admonishing look as she breezed out of the kitchen.

Holland laughed. The starving part was probably true. But Chloe and Tristan's house was one of the few places where she and Myles could just hang out on a Saturday night and not hide their relationship. Or at least they could for another half hour.

Rina and Scott, Zurie and Mace, and Layla and Bastian were arriving soon for dinner.

Laughter echoed from outside, and Holland followed Myles's glance to the side window. Tristan and Chloe were standing on the deck having an animated conversation. The couple pointed at each other. Tristan grabbed her hand and pulled her in for a kiss.

Myles tossed a tomato up in the air and caught it. "Chloe said this is couples' night?"

"Yes." Holland slipped the tomato from his hand.

"And what's the explanation for us being here?"

"We're two single people visiting town and they feel sorry for us."

He grimaced. "Wow. That's almost the same as being stuck at the kids' table."

"It's not that bad. Other people here tonight might not know we're a couple, but we do and that's what counts."

"You're right." Myles carefully slipped the knife out of Holland's hand, grasped her waist and turned her to face him.

She rested her hands on his chest. "What are you doing?"

He leaned in. "Stocking up on reminders of us to get me through the night."

Sparks ignited as soon as Myles's lips touched hers. Holland pressed against him, and Myles glided downward, cupping her curves, melding them together.

Lost in the slow drift and glide of delicious pleasure, they didn't hear Chloe and Tristan walk in until Chloe cleared her throat.

"Okay," her best friend said. "Tristan, I think it's time for Myles to see the horses."

Myles let go of Holland. "But I'm helping with dinner."

"No. We're helping you." Tristan clapped Myles on the shoulder and steered him out of the kitchen. "You need a change of scenery."

Chloe stared at Holland. "Wow! I can only imagine what would have happened if you two were alone."

The heat of self-consciousness replaced some of the heat of desire in Holland's cheeks. "We got a little caught up."

"Well, you have about ten minutes to get *uncaught* before everyone shows up. Myles is definitely going to need more time."

As Holland watched Myles and Tristan walk across the back lawn toward a small stable in the distance, the reality of why she and Myles had been separated pushed out a breath. "Yeah, we need to watch our behavior tonight."

"Don't worry. Tristan and I will help keep you in line." Chloe leaned back on the counter and faced her. "Or you could just put it out there tonight and tell everyone to keep it to themselves."

"I don't know…" Holland worried her bottom lip.

"Relax, okay? You can trust Tristan's family. Our secret engagement and surprise wedding wouldn't have happened without them."

"But it's not just your family that will be here."

"That's right. Layla and Bastian are coming." Chloe shrugged. "But from what I heard, they had to deal with a secret or two in their relationship. Still, I can understand wanting to be cautious." She tipped her head toward the window. "How is Myles handling the situation?"

"It's not easy for him. I drop by the house when workers aren't there, which is hardly ever, and I don't stay long. The other day, he mentioned meeting up at Rina's café for a cup of coffee but pretending we just bumped into each other." She sighed regretfully. "I was really tempted to take him up on that but ultimately turned him down. He was disappointed, and I was, too. It would have been nice just to sit and talk or walk around the town square holding hands. And the hardest part is, we can't even spend the night together."

"But Myles's house is so remote. You could probably get away with driving out there to see him."

"And what happens if someone notices *your* car sitting in Myles's driveway in the middle of the night?"

Chloe winced. "No. That wouldn't be good." Her face lit up with a conspiratorial smile. "But I could drop you off at his place for a sleepover, or we could sneak Myles into the guesthouse."

"I like the idea of a sleepover." Holland gave a

rueful laugh as she moved on to slicing cucumbers. "But I would have to be the one doing the sneaking. Myles would do it, but he wouldn't be thrilled. I wouldn't be able to enjoy the moment knowing he felt that way."

"How long do they want to keep the engagement with Nash on the front burner?"

"Until at least a week after the movie wraps." Holland cut the ends from a cucumber. "But that's longer than Myles and I will be here in Bolan together." Sadness and frustration mingled inside her. According to what she'd blocked out on her schedule, she was only supposed to be in Bolan for another ten days. He was supposed to head home, too. They'd talked about seeing if they could squeeze in another week or so. Myles could, but she had meetings in LA. She was considering rescheduling them. Or flying there and coming back.

But even with the extended time, they would still have to keep their relationship a secret. They hadn't broached the topic of continuing to see each other long distance. She just didn't know how she felt about it. Bi-coastal relationships were hard to navigate. Sydney and Jake's situation was an example of that.

The doorbell rang.

Chloe patted Holland's arm. "Let me know if you want to do the sleepover plan with you at his place. I have a black catsuit that's perfect for the occasion."

"*Catsuit?* You're just dropping me off at his house, not burglarizing it."

"The catsuit isn't for your sleepover." Chloe gave

a coy smile. "It's for mine when I come back home and play catch-me-if-you-can with Tristan."

Full from a delicious dinner of grilled chicken, roast potatoes, salad and generous amounts of wine for the non–designated drivers, the couples chatted at the table.

Chloe and Tristan sat at the ends of the large oval while the rest of the duos sat across from each other. Keeping the partners separated on what was supposed to be couples' night was an odd seating arrangement, but no one seemed to notice it. The flow of conversation had been continuous, and everyone was having a good time.

And in some ways, it was like the kids' table for Holland and Myles. They were on either side of Chloe, and she'd been keeping an eye on them.

But Holland had been good about not looking at him. At least, not too often.

As she drank iced tea, she met Myles's gaze. He gave her a small smile, and like gravity, it was hard to pull away. She just wanted to kiss him, hold him without holding back. And spend the rest of the night in bed with him.

"Holland." Chloe tapped her arm. "How are things going with your research? Have you found any houses with interesting stories for your documentary?"

She swallowed her sip of iced tea. "The house with the wine seller is a possibility, but it's not very compelling. Honestly, the most interesting thing I've come across is the letter Myles and I discovered in his fireplace."

"Really?" Mace asked. "When did this happen?"

As all attention swung her direction, it was easy to read Chloe's raised-brow expression. She was questioning why Holland had put herself in direct association with Myles.

Myles chimed in. "When I first got here, some of the front bricks on the mantel had fallen off, and it was tucked in a secret compartment. It was a love letter. After hearing about Holland's project that night at Pasture Lane, it seemed like something she would be interested in pursuing."

Holland smiled inwardly. That wasn't quite what happened, but it was the perfect save.

"Who wrote the letter?" Zurie asked.

Holland responded, "There aren't any names on it, just initials. It's to B, from L, and the writer is begging B to run away with him. They met at the flea market fair and started secretly seeing each other. But she was engaged."

"That sounds familiar," Chloe muttered, obviously referring to Nash and Gina.

Holland gave her a look.

Chloe drank from her wineglass and feigned innocence.

"But the engagement wasn't a love match." Holland added. "She was marrying the other guy because of her parents."

Compassion shown in Rina's eyes. "So this couple cared about each other, but they couldn't be together? That must have been difficult."

The comment struck home for Holland and a rush of melancholy hit. Not being able to touch Myles or just acknowledge what she felt for him in front of people, like now, was really hard.

Afraid someone would see how she felt on her face, Holland quickly focused on rearranging the napkin on her lap. But she lost her place in the story.

"It was really difficult for the guy," Myles interjected. "He saw her as a bridesmaid in someone's wedding. Watching her walk down the aisle reminded him of what was coming. It's kind of hard not to empathize with him"

As he picked up where she left off, Holland felt another rush. This time it was relief. She glanced up and briefly met his gaze. The understanding she saw in his eyes, what it for her or L?

Remembering the rest of what the letter said, Holland refocused on the group. "Apparently, after the wedding they met up in the church courtyard, and she tore her blue dress running away from him. He'd planned on keeping the torn fabric as a memento, but it was too painful for him. He enclosed it in the letter. He'd decided to leave town. But the last sentence in the letter was a final plea for her to come with him."

"Well." Zurie chuckled. "The guy definitely wasn't short on drama."

"Aww," Rina said. "Don't be so heartless. It was a tough situation to be in and he was really in love."

"Yeah," Scott added. "With an engaged woman.

By getting involved with her, he was just setting himself up to get burned."

Myles frowned briefly with a contemplative expression as he took a sip of his tea.

"I'm with Scott," Mace said. "But sometimes women drive men to do insane things."

"Oh really?" Zurie replied. "Does that include you?"

Smiling, Mace winked. "You only make me do insanely good things."

Zurie's face glowed.

"Okay, you two," Rina gave them a lighthearted scolding. "Save that dirty talk for when you get home."

Everyone laughed as the couple playfully made eyes at each other.

As the chuckles died down, Tristan frowned pensively. "The flea market fair—didn't those used to just happen in the summer?" He looked to Rina and Zurie.

"I think so," Rina replied. "The last one I remembering going to was when I was in elementary school, maybe younger? I don't think they continued much longer after that."

Holland turned to Myles. His brow rose a fraction. Were they thinking the same thing? The property records plus knowing when the fair took place could narrow the time frame.

"The ownership documents for the house?" Bastian asked. "I'm assuming you already checked the records at town hall for anyone with those initials?"

"Yes. And I had my attorney pull the records." Myles shrugged. "No matches showed up."

"And that was so disappointing," Holland added. "I should have guessed it wouldn't be that easy."

"I hope you find answers," Rina said. "I'm dying to know if they ran off together or if B stayed and got married."

Later that night, as Holland lay in bed, the discussion at dinner about the letter played through her mind.

Along with Myles secretly blowing her a kiss before she walked out the front door of Chloe and Tristan's house.

Myles had been ready to leave, too, along with Zurie and Mace, but Tristan had snagged Myles before he walked out. Probably part of Chloe's plan to keep them both in line.

Her phone buzzed with a text on the bedside table, and she picked it up.

Good night, beautiful.

The text from Myles made her happy and a little sad. She missed him so much.

If they had left Chloe and Tristan's house at the same time, it would have been so easy to follow him home and finish that kiss they'd shared in the kitchen. So many times that night, whenever they'd gotten close, she'd been tempted to just touch him.

Like after dinner, when they'd all gone on a moonlit stroll to the stable. Everyone except for her and

Myles had been holding hands or had their arms wrapped around each other.

At one point, Myles's arm had brushed hers, and just as she was about to loop one finger with his, Chloe had appeared out of nowhere and surreptitiously nudged her along.

She couldn't be mad at her friend. That had been the right thing to do, but...

A hint of the disappointment Holland had felt a few times at dinner that night hit her now. She could honestly relate to the torture L had expressed in his letters to his love.

What about Myles? Did he feel the same way?

Holland started to call and ask him that question. But then she stopped. What was the point of sharing her misery? Especially if they couldn't do anything about it. Her choices were the ones that now kept them apart.

And maybe Myles was starting to have doubts?

At dinner, after Scott had made the comment about L setting himself up by getting involved with an engaged woman, she'd seen the look that passed over Myles's face.

She and Nash weren't really engaged, but like a few things that resonated as everyone had discussed the letter at dinner, maybe Myles worried that he was setting himself up to get burned?

After a long moment, Holland finally responded.

Good night. XOXO

She couldn't speak for Myles, but she knew in her gut that even for the short-term, or longer if they decided to take a leap of faith and try a long distance relationship, being with him was worth any potential pain down the line. Closing her eyes, she imagined Myles kissing her, holding her.

This constant separation—could they survive it? Or like with L and B, would it threaten to drive them apart?

Chapter Fifteen

A few days later, as Holland ate a bagel and drank coffee in the kitchen, she went over her plan of where to start narrowing the time frame of the letter—the flea market fair.

Setting her breakfast aside, she went to her laptop on the counter and searched the internet. As a social event in the area, it had probably been announced in the local paper. And from what she could find, the main periodical in town was the *Bolan Town Talk*.

According to the blog's website, it had been around since 1941. Maybe it had been a physical paper before becoming a blog?

The one person who could most likely provide the quickest answer to that question, along with where past editions of the paper might exist, was the blog's current main writer and owner—Anna Ashford.

An unease when it came to talking to reporters made Holland hesitate in picking up her phone. What if Anna kept up with entertainment news? Would the woman start questioning her about Nash and the possible engagement?

Knowing she had to take the chance if she wanted answers about the letter, Holland started to dial the number listed on the website. She figured if the reporter asked her any personal questions about Nash, her answer would simply be "no comment."

But before the call connected, she had second thoughts about using her personal phone. Her number would show up as private, but still, these days finding out people's information was so easy. And Anna was the last person she wanted to have access to her number.

Holland quickly hung up and decided to use the landline in the office instead.

The call picked up on the third ring. *"Bolan Town Talk.* Senior reporter Anna Ashford speaking."

"Good morning, Anna. This is Holland Ainsley."

"Miss Ainsley… Holland. What a surprise. How may I help you?" There was a rustling sound, as if Anna was quickly moving things around.

A vision sprang in her mind of the woman grabbing pen and paper so she could write down the upcoming conversation—or maybe she was scrambling for a recording device.

Holland took a deep breath and put a smile in her voice. "I was wondering if there are any past editions of the *Bolan Town Talk* anywhere from around twenty years ago?"

"Yes. It was a local paper back then. You can find them in the archives office at city hall."

"Thanks so much. I'll give them a call right now."

"You need my authorization to see them." Anna said the words as if she were dangling a carrot, clearly wanting something in return.

Holland stayed professional. "Would you mind giving me that authorization, then? I'd really appreciate it."

"So you need to see the archives for the research you're doing?"

"Yes, that's it."

"And this research, it's for a documentary. Not the sequel to *Shadow Valley*?"

Not talking about the future of *Shadow Valley* sequels was part of the agreement Holland had signed with her former partners. "I'm sorry, but I can't comment on what's happening with that movie. About that authorization...would it be possible for you to call the archive department now?"

"Yes, that's doable."

"Wonderful. I really appreciate your help."

"Sure. One more question about *Shadow Valley*..."

Holland's cell phone rang on the desk. "Sorry to cut this short, but my office is calling. I really have to go. Thanks again for your help with the authorization, Anna. Bye." Holland hung up.

Shoot. Was she too abrupt? Hopefully not. Otherwise, the reporter might not make that authorization.

Releasing a long breath, she answered her phone. "Hello."

"Hi, Holland…it's Layla. We met at Chloe and Tristan's the other night. Is this a bad time?"

"No, not at all. How are you? I enjoyed meeting you and Bastian."

"We're fine. Bastian and I were just talking about how we enjoyed meeting you, and hearing about your documentary. Actually, the documentary, that's why I'm calling. The dress shop Bastian's grandmother owns has been here for years. Chances are, Charlotte dressed the bride for the wedding mentioned in your letter."

Holland's pulse skittered with excitement. Another promising lead. That was good news. "Do you think she'll remember the brides from that far back?"

"She probably won't remember offhand, but she still has alteration records from back then. You might find something. I'm happy to help you look."

"That would be fantastic! I'm going by the archive department this morning. I'm hoping to find something about the flea market fair in one of the old editions of the local newspaper. If I can find out when the last fair happened, we could work our way back from that year."

"Sounds good. Call me when you know more, and we can set up a time to dig through the Charlotte's records."

Less than an hour later, Holland drove past a sign

proclaiming, Welcome to Bolan. Friends and Smiles for Miles Live Here.

She could add her own smile to the count with all the locals who lived there. Encouraged by Layla's news, she couldn't wait to do a records dive. She'd even called Myles to give him a quick update. He hadn't picked up, but she'd left a voice mail about everything.

Truthfully, she'd just wanted to hear his voice. But he was probably busy working on the house. Maybe they could catch up with each other later? She sure hoped so.

Merging with light traffic, she drove around the square searching for a parking space and found one near the flower shop. Buttons & Lace Boutique was across the square on the other side of the street.

Some pedestrians leisurely window-shopped or strolled through the square, while others in business attire and uniforms darted in and out of businesses.

Bolan city hall was toward the edge of town. It didn't take long to make the walk to the two-story brick building with white trim. The clock in the tower on the roof indicated it was almost nine thirty.

Holland opened the heavy wood door and stepped inside. The cool, light-tiled lobby was empty. She crossed the wide corridor and approached the woman sitting behind the glass at the reception counter.

"Hello, I'm looking for the archives department."

The older woman looked over her glasses at Holland. "Archives, hold on a moment." She dialed an extension on the phone next to her. "I thought I saw

Bindy leave earlier." Seconds passed as she held the receiver to her ear. She hung up. "She's not there. It's gone to voice mail."

"Do you know when she'll be back?"

"No. Since there weren't any appointments, she left to run errands. Bindy's retired, and this a part-time job." The woman waved away her own comment. "We let her do what she wants. For what she's paid, it almost qualifies as a volunteer position. If you leave your number, I'll have her call if she comes back."

Not when Bindy came back, but *if*.

Holland gave the woman her office number. As she trudged out the building, she called her assistant in LA to make her aware that Bindy might call. Anna must have just missed Bindy when she called to give authorization.

Now what? Holland took in the town square. She could check in with Layla about the alteration records. Without a narrower date range, it might be the equivalent of looking for a needle in a haystack. Or maybe she'd get lucky.

Taking the long way through the square, Holland arrived at the boutique with a glass storefront and opened the door with *Buttons & Lace* stenciled on it.

Inside, racks of clothing interspersed with floor-length mirrors lined the side walls. Folded shirts and other tops were neatly stacked on displays in the center of the space.

Up ahead, Layla stood at the cashier station ring-ing up purchases for a couple of women. She acknowledged Holland with a nod and a smile.

Purses on a wall rack caught her eye. She sifted through them, but she wasn't in the mood to shop. The possibility of finding answers about the letter remained at the top of her mind.

Last night, Rina had voiced what Holland was most interested in finding out—did L and B break up or did they find happiness together?

Smiling, Layla joined her at the purse rack. "Hi. I didn't think I would see you for hours. I imagined you buried under a stack of old newspapers."

"Unfortunately, I didn't get that far. The person who works in archives wasn't there. According to the woman at the main desk, she might not come back to work for the rest of the day."

"Oh no." Layla gave her an empathetic look. "That's so disappointing. I know you were looking forward to searching the papers."

"Maybe I'll get lucky and the archives lady will come back. Since I'm in waiting mode, I was wondering if I could search through the alteration records, maybe starting at twenty-five years ago?"

"I wish you could, but they're in Charlotte's attic at the house."

An attractive older woman with a silvery-blond bob, dressed in slim sky blue pants and a loose black pullover, joined them by the rack.

Layla turned to the woman. "Charlotte, this is Holland Ainsley. I mentioned her to you this morning. Holland, this is Charlotte Henry."

Charlotte patted Holland's arm. "I know exactly who you are. When you were in town with the movie, I'd see you walking around, and I couldn't help but admire your style. Especially those combat boots. You made them look good with everything."

"Thank you."

"So Layla said you're making a documentary and my alteration records might help?"

"Yes…" Holland explained about the documentary and the letter.

"Oh, that *is* interesting." Charlotte's blue eyes lit up. "I wonder who it could be. You said there was a piece of torn cloth from a dress. Do happened to have it with you?"

"I do."

"Let me see it. Hang on, I need my glasses." Charlotte motioned for Layla and Holland to follow her.

At the cashier's station, she took a pair of wireframe glasses from a drawer and put them on.

Holland took the plastic sleeve from her backpack and handed it to Charlotte.

The older woman glanced at the letter, then peered at the lace-edged cloth. "This looks like my work. May I take it out of this sleeve?"

"Yes, go ahead." If Charlotte recognized her work, maybe… Holland controlled her excitement. She shouldn't get her hopes up.

Charlotte examined the fabric from both sides. "Oh, yes. This is definitely my work. Nice and neat." She showed it to Layla. "See the stitching connecting the lace? You want it to be sturdy but not overdone where it's noticeable. Too many seamstresses think that because no one will get a close-up look, it doesn't matter. But it's about skill and craftsmanship."

A customer walked in, and Layla went to assist them.

Going out on a limb, Holland asked Charlotte, "You wouldn't happen to remember making a dress that might match this cloth?"

"Oh no." Charlotte laughed as she carefully slipped the fabric back into the sleeve on the counter. "Just looking at it, I couldn't. But if you can pinpoint the year of the wedding in the letter, it might jog my memory."

"I'd planned to look up when the flea market fair took place in past newspapers in the town archives, but the clerk who runs the office wasn't there. Anna Ashford said she'd call in an authorization. Hopefully, the clerk will have it and I can start searching."

"You don't need an authorization. You just walk in, tell Bindy what you want, and she'll find it."

"But then why would Anna tell me that?"

"Does she know about your research?"

"Yes. But not the specifics or about this letter."

"That explains it. She was going to have Bindy pump you for information to support the so-called authorization." Charlotte harrumphed. "Bindy knows better than to get involved with Anna's foolishness."

And the woman was a town employee. Wasn't doing something like that unethical? But the woman at the main window had said they let Bindy do what she wanted.

"Well, now I now," Holland said. "Thanks for the heads-up."

"You're welcome." As Holland put the letter away, Charlotte pointed at it. "Seeing that line about the flea market fair sure brought back memories. I had a booth at the event the first year. It was held in a dirt field downwind of the pastures at the dairy farm. Between the dust, the flies and the smell of cow manure, it was miserable, and year after year, from what I heard, it never improved." She shook her head. "A few years later, they added carnival rides as a last-ditch effort to drum up interest, but it didn't work. Someone finally paved it after the dairy farm closed, but it's still called Dairy Field. One of the customers mentioned that there's an antique bazaar or something happening there this month."

"Dairy Field. I'll remember that for my search. Thanks for your time."

"You're welcome. Give us a call when you have the dates, and between the three of us, we'll find what you're looking for."

Holland waved goodbye to Layla and walked out of the store. She figured she should still hang around town in case the archives office opened back up.

A couple passed by, carrying iced coffees topped with whipped cream and caramel.

Her mouth started to water. Having a coffee drink at Brewed Haven and working on her laptop was the perfect way to spend a couple of hours.

Hiking the straps of her backpack farther on her shoulders, she walked toward the café.

As she got closer, a line of people walked out the door.

One of them was Myles.

His gray shirt and jeans fit him in all the right ways. He was about to slip on a pair of sunglasses when his gaze connected with hers. The exact coffee drink she craved was in his hands.

Myles strolled over to her. "Hi."

"Hello."

He looked as lost for words as she was. Or maybe the words weren't lost. They just couldn't say what they wanted to each other.

Myles pointed to the small iced coffee. "This came with the breakfast. I decided to take it to go."

"I was just about to grab one of those myself."

"Take mine. I haven't touched it."

Take me...

She'd give up coffee drinks for at least a decade for a kiss. But right then, her only choice was iced coffee—his or going inside to get one. She wasn't ready to stop talking to him yet.

"Thank you." Holland slipped the iced coffee from his hand and took a long sip. It was good.

Myles dropped his gaze to her mouth and stared.

She swiped her tongue over her bottom lip and tasted whipped cream and caramel. "I'm being so messy right now." As she lifted her hand to wipe it away, Myles reached out as if to do it.

He stopped himself. As he dropped his hand, a hint of frustration crossed his face.

A bottleneck formed in front of the café as more people walked out and others waited to get inside.

Myles glanced around. "We're in the way."

Holland moved with him, and they kept walking as she sipped her drink. They probably shouldn't be together like this. But couldn't they just be two people walking down the street, having a friendly conversation?

"Are you on your way to pick something up for the house?" she asked.

"No, I was just catching up with Scott. He might have time to help me work on a few more things. We had breakfast to talk about it."

"I was wondering why you didn't call me. No... wait. That didn't come out right. I figured you were busy. And I'm really happy he's helping you out."

Myles chuckled. "I get it. I missed you, too. And I was bummed that I missed your call. Did you find what you were looking for in the archives?"

"No. The office is closed." She told him about her conversation with Charlotte, then about Anna and the situation with Bindy.

When she finished, he shook his head in disbelief. "Bindy was going to spy on you for Anna? She works for the town. That's not ethical."

"Exactly." One more thing to add to the list of what they agreed on. Did they even have a list? Maybe they should. Iced coffee was good. Kissing was good. She really needed to stop thinking about kissing. Or what it would feel like to make love to him again.

As they stood, waiting to cross the street, a blue tour van passed them.

Myles pointed and read the words scrolling across a digital monitor on the side of it. "*Dairy Field*. Isn't that where you said Charlotte mentioned the flea market fair used to be?"

"Yes, that's the place. There's an event going on there. Something to do with antiques."

"Seeing that bus has to be a sign." Myles's slow, gorgeous smile sparked her curiosity and had her heartbeat racing at the same time.

She couldn't help but smile back at him. "For what?"

"For you to run away with me."

Chapter Sixteen

"What?" Holland laughed. "How are we escaping and where are we running away to?"

Myles pointed. "We're playing tourists and escaping where that bus takes us. It's just a day trip."

"You're serious?"

"As serious as you are about iced coffee."

Yes, let's go...

That's what Myles wanted Holland to say, but he wouldn't coerce or try to force her into it. More than anything, he just wanted a few hours with her, away from anything to do with houses or other people. He wanted a moment to be just about the two of them.

She'd accepted the iced coffee and she'd walked halfway down the street with him, not worried about who saw them. But maybe this impulsive idea was too much of a risk.

Holland glanced down the street, then back at him. The expression on her face had *ready to play hooky* written all over it.

"We might have to make a run for it." Myles glanced at the half-empty cup in her hand.

Holland tossed the coffee in a nearby trash can. "Let's do it."

They waited for traffic to pass before dashing across the street.

Maybe he should run ahead to make sure the bus didn't leave without them. Holland might need to walk at a slower pace. It hadn't been that long since she'd bruised her hip.

As they hurried across the town square, she took the lead. Laughing, she glanced back at him.

Her radiant smile hit Myles square in the chest, and he stumbled, giving her more of a lead.

Holland called out, "Keep up, slow poke!"

Right now, his heart felt like it was about to beat out of his chest from pure happiness. Her joy was like fresh air to his lungs. He couldn't get enough of it.

They reached the bookstore slightly out of breath.

Myles approached the dark-haired woman standing at the open door of the half-empty tour bus. "Excuse me. Do you have room for two more people?"

"I sure do. You just need to hurry up and purchase your tickets in the bookstore. We leave in ten minutes. One of you can hop in the van and grab your seats."

"Thanks. We'll do that." Myles looked to Holland. "Go ahead and get on. I'll buy the tickets."

He hurried inside. A mindless adventure was just what he and Holland needed.

Holland stepped onto the tour bus. The aisle divided the coach into two rows of double seats.

The tourists sitting on the bus were spread out. All of them had at least three decades on her and Myles.

Some of the empty seats had laminated signs on them that said Occupied. None of available seats were side by side. She and Myles would have to split up.

A seat next to an older, balding gentleman holding a duffel bag to his chest was available. But as she approached him, he scowled at her, and she moved on. Toward the back, two older women sat in the window seats in the opposite aisle.

Holland smiled at both of them. "Are these spots available?"

"They sure are. Have a seat." The brassy redhead on the right patted the space next to her. The woman's round cheeks were almost the same crimson as her lipstick.

The redhead glanced at the Black woman with her hair in a neat salt-and-pepper bun across the aisle who had her eyes closed. "Here." She handed Holland a canvas tote bag filled with more cloth bags. "Put that in the seat next to Dora so no one will try to take it."

Holland complied and sat down.

"I'm Aggie." The redhead smiled. "You met Dora. Or at least you will when she wakes up. The one who gave you the stink eye is Oliver, but don't mind him. He only has two emotions—grumpy and grumpier."

"Hello, I'm Holland."

"Nice to meet you, Holland. You're very pretty."

"Thank you." Holland tucked her backpack between her feet.

"Are you single? Dora and I both have grandsons that are available."

"I'm…" How in the world did she answer that question? *I'm almost fake engaged and I'm currently running away with my secret boyfriend?*

More people filed onto the bus, including Myles.

Aggie nudged Holland with her elbow. "Is he the one you're saving other seat for?"

"Yes, that's my friend Myles."

"Oh…a *friend*." Aggie winked. "I used to have a few of those, too, back in my day. Hand me my bag."

Holland gave the woman her canvas tote back.

Myles reached her seat and pointed to the empty one across the aisle from Holland. "Is this one mine?"

The way Aggie was eyeing him with appreciation made it hard for Holland to suppress a chuckle. "Uh-huh."

He sat down.

Dora woke up and blinked several times as if she thought she was seeing things. Smiling, she sat up straighter in the seat and patted her hair. "Hello."

Myles gave the two older women a polite nod. "Hi, ladies."

"Hi, I'm Aggie and that's Dora, and you are?"

"I'm Myles."

"And you're handsome." Dora smiled. "If you're single, I've got a grandniece about your age."

Aggie pointed between Holland and Myles. "They're…friends."

Dora's brow rose. "Oh, I see. Would you two like to sit together?"

"We're fine," Holland insisted.

"No, we're good," Myles added at the same time.

"Aggie." Dora motioned. "Come sit with me. I need a window seat."

"I know." Aggie stood, holding her bag of bags. "Sitting in an aisle seat makes you nauseous."

Dora gave a subtle eyeroll. "Can you say that louder? I don't think the people walking down the street heard you."

Aggie crowded into Holland's space, giving her no choice but to grab her backpack and get out of the way. "Nausea, indigestion, it's nothing to be ashamed of. Everyone gets it. Even him."

Myles stood, too. Like Holland, he'd obviously been raised to respect his elders. But like her, he was having a hard time keeping a smile from his face as they listened to the two women go back and forth.

As Aggie pushed past, she bumped Holland into Myles.

He grasped Holland's shoulders, helping to steady her. But she felt far from stable with him looking down at her.

His mouth was so close, even with her backpack squashed between them, all she had to do was rise on her toes, and—

"Everyone, take their seats, please." The dark-haired woman, who'd been standing by the door, was now behind the wheel, revving up the engine of the van.

Holland scooted into the window seat Aggie had abandoned, and Myles sat next to her. His hard thigh pressed against hers. Being this close went against all the rules she'd set for them being together in public, and so did interlacing their hands resting on the seat between them.

But it felt so good to break the rules. Just this once.

A half hour later, Myles helped Aggie and Dora off the bus.

The two women—mainly Aggie—had chatted with him and Holland the whole way.

Almost everyone riding the bus, outside of him and Holland, lived in a subdivision for residents over fifty of mostly townhomes about an hour and a half outside Bolan. They regularly took the tour bus to events at Dairy Field that ranged from flea markets and car shows to concerts and events like today's bazaar, featuring local and visiting dealers specializing in antique and vintage items.

He'd been grateful to have the older women as a distraction. Otherwise, he would have just obsessed over the way Holland had looked at him as they'd stood in the aisle waiting for Aggie to sit back down.

He'd never been the caveman type, but a part of him had wanted to throw Holland over his shoulder, get off the bus and find a place where he could taste, touch and explore every inch of her until they'd sated their need for one another.

As most of the group from the bus hurried into the crowd, including Dora, Aggie lagged behind.

The former event planner considered herself an expert on all the events at Dairy Field and wanted to give them the inside scoop.

She elbowed Myles in the side and pointed to the square paved area surrounded by grass and few trees in the distance. "Those large white tents over there are where the dealers are located. Food is on the left. Stick to the Sommersby Farm Vineyard station. They serve good portions for the money, and they're good with sanitation. Pasture Lane Restaurant from Tillbridge is excellent, too, but it doesn't look like they're here today. The porta potties are way back there, so don't wait too long to go. And don't be late for the bus. It leaves exactly at four thirty."

"Thanks for the tips," Holland said.

"Absolutely." Aggie pointed as she walked away. "You two have fun."

Myles turned to Holland. "Where should we start? Food or the dealers' tents?"

"Let's start with the dealers first." Holland slid on her backpack. But instead of coming closer to hold his hand, she moved away.

They were back to keeping their distance. Which didn't sit right with him. But they *were* together. He'd have to remain content with just that for the next three and half hours.

In the first tent, they both gravitated toward a collection of stained glass windows.

Holland pointed to ones with a floral pattern. "I could see those in your dining room. The light reflecting through the curved windows would be absolutely stunning."

Myles could easily envision what she described.

As they walked though other rows with furniture, they found they liked the same styles—solid pieces made from natural and dark wood.

In the second tent, multiple items were being sold. He glanced over at an assortment of silverware and colorful dishware. And saw there was also a selection of musical instruments and picture frames.

Some items were funny, like the ceramic cow salt and pepper shakers. One of the cartoonish-looking animals had a bow tie on, while the other had a ribbon on top of its head.

They each took close-up pictures with them.

He held the cow shakers up and pretended they were boxing each other.

She struck a pose, holding them up to her ears like earrings.

And there were items that weren't easily identifiable to them. Myles held up a metal rod with brackets on the end of it. "I think it's a back scratcher."

"What? No." Holland took it from him. "You could end up knocking yourself out just trying get it over your shoulder. It's a stand of some kind. See?" She set it on the floor, and it wobbled. "Or maybe not."

"Excuse me, sir." Myles flagged down a man at the end of the stall. "Can you settle an argument, please? I think this is a back scratcher. My girlfriend says it's a stand."

The man laughed. They were both wrong. The dealer explained what it was, but Myles barely heard a word.

Girlfriend. That's what he'd just called Holland. He hadn't used that word for anyone in his life for a very long time. It had just rolled out of him naturally. And Holland hadn't looked at him funny. But couples having a friendly disagreement could often be humorous, and maybe she just thought he was playing into the moment. But he liked the thought of one day being able introduce her as that to his friends or Dante in the future.

They hadn't talked about if there could be a future for them outside of Bolan. But everytime he thought about time running out for them, he wanted more of it. And he just didn't want time without PDA restrictions. He wanted time without the restrictions of a time limit. Time that would just unfold in front of them. Did she want that, too?

My girlfriend, Holland...

As they walked away, Holland laughed. "Lightning rods? I didn't see that answer coming."

Myles reluctantly nudged aside the thought in his mind. Focusing on the now was important. "I know. Neither did I."

They looked around a bit longer then decided to take a break. Neither of them was really interested in picking up anything. Holland didn't have room in her suitcase, and he had enough things in his apartment in New York.

Outside, they ate where Aggie had suggested, feasting on fresh bread, along with a plate of Roma tomatoes, fresh mozzarella and basil drizzled with olive oil. They also bought white wine to drink that had been made at the vineyard.

They talked, ate, and sat in companionable silence.

As Holland swirled the last bit of bread in the olive oil, she had a dreamy look on her face.

He gently nudged her foot under the table with his. "What are you thinking about?"

She looked at him from underneath her lashes. "How much I'm enjoying running away with you. Thank you for suggesting this."

His chest swelled a little. It made him happy to make her happy. "Well running away is something I thought a rule-breaker like you might want to do."

"Oh really?" Holland gave him a coy look. "Are you trying to sweet talk me or impress me?"

"Both." He leaned closer, barely resisting the urge to close the distance and kiss her. "How am I doing do far?"

"On a scale of one-to-ten? She feigned contemplation. "I haven't made my mind up yet."

On the way back to the tents, he saw another rule-breaking opportunity as they passed a couple of concession trailers not in use.

He snagged her hand and quickly led her in back of them.

Holland gave him a quizzical look. "The tents are that way. What are we doing here."

"I'm helping you make up our mind." After double that no one was around, Myles brought her close and kissed her.

Releasing a soft moan, she slid her free hand up his chest and around his nape, joining in for a deepening kiss.

Her taste, the way her soft curves fit against him was more potent than the wine they'd just consumed.

Both needing air they broke apart.

She leaned her forehead to his chest and laughed. "Okay. You earned it. Ten"

Reluctant to leave, he took her hand, and they walked back to the front of the trailers.

Just before they got there she slipped her hand from his.

A small space opened in his chest, registering the loss.

Holland's phone chimed. She paused and took it from her bag and answered it. "Hello. Hi…no, I'm actually at Dairy Field. Really?" Holland's eyes widened as she looked to him. "Sure, I'll come as soon as I get back."

She ended the call.

"Was that Bindy?"

"No, it was Charlotte." Excitement sparked in her eyes. "She's discovered something about the letter."

Chapter Seventeen

Holland followed Myles off the bus along with members of the group who needed to refresh themselves before continuing to their final stop.

As she got off the bus in front of the bookstore, Holland accepted a bottled water from the driver, who was passing them out to the group.

The return trip from Dairy Field had seemed so much longer than the one going there. Most likely it was because she'd been anxious to return to the dress boutique.

But she had also been torn about ending her adventure with Myles. He'd mentioned wanting to impress her and had more than just succeeded. Especially with that kiss behind the trailers. The way he was going, he could almost sweet talk her into anything.

It was no wonder the two women on the bus were enamored with him.

On the sidewalk, Holland and Myles said their goodbyes to Aggie and Dora. Both women had brought back multiple purchases from their trip.

Dora went inside the bookstore, while Aggie remained outside to keep an eye on their purchases.

"It was good to have some younger folks on the trip," Aggie said. "You should join us for the next one. I don't remember what it is. I've been meaning to grab an itinerary for this tour and a few others I'm interested in. Well, shoot, I don't have my readers on." She glanced up at Myles with a slightly pitiful look. "And the print is so small on those things."

Smiling, he took the hint and offered the woman his arm. "I'll go with you."

"Oh, would you?" The older woman slipped her arm through his.

He looked to Holland. "I know you need to go. Do you want me to call you later?"

Wait. No hug or kiss on the cheek? Of course not. They weren't hidden behind a trailer at Dairy Field. They were back in Bolan standing on a public sidewalk. "Do you have time to meet me at the boutique when you're done here?"

"Well, of course he does," Aggie chimed in. "We'll just be a minute."

Myles's eyes held humor has he glanced at Aggie and then back to Holland. "I'll be there."

Holland paused a moment, watching Myles walk

with Aggie into the store, before she headed across the square.

He was strong and patient in every way. Perfect boyfriend material. At the bazaar, when Myles had told the dealer she was his girlfriend, she'd been surprised, but her heart had skipped beats with happiness. But she'd held back on acknowledging what he'd said. It could have just been a slip of the tongue or Myles feeding into the fun moment of asking the dealer to settle a pretend argument between them.

But for a brief moment, it had made her wonder again, that if the situation with Nash wasn't currently in their way, could they make a real relationship work outside of Bolan? But were they ready for that after knowing each other for such a short time?

Shaking off the question she didn't have an answer to yet, Holland focused on the task at hand. She entered Buttons & Lace Boutique. Charlotte was at the counter.

"Perfect timing," She passed by Holland. "I don't have any customers." She locked the door and flipped over a Be Back Soon sign.

"Myles will here in a minute." Seeing a puzzled expression on Charlotte's face, Holland added, "He's the owner of the house where the letter was found. And he's a friend."

"Oh, I see." The older woman's brow rose like Aggie's and Dora's had on the bus. "While we're waiting for him, would you help me tidy up a bit?"

"Of course." Holland helped Charlotte fold shirts on the middle display. "Will Layla be joining us?"

"No." A guarded look briefly came over the boutique owner's face. "She had some things to take care of with Bastian, so I sent her home early."

Something was wrong. Charlotte was still friendly, but she also seemed tense.

Just as Holland was about to call Myles for an ETA, he showed up at the door.

The older woman let him in, and he introduced himself.

Doors locked, they walked to the cashier's counter.

Wanting to break through the tension, Holland said., "I appreciate you helping me with this."

"Don't thank me yet." Charlotte went behind the counter. She pulled a folder out of the drawer and laid it in front of her. "This may open an entire can of worms."

Myles moved closer to Holland. "How so?"

"It'll become clearer in a minute. Trust me." Charlotte looked directly at Holland. "When I went home for lunch this afternoon, I tracked down Bindy and told her my tax dollars didn't pay her a salary for running personal errands or trying to bamboozle people. And if she didn't want me to raise hell at the next town hall meeting about it, she needed get back to her office and find the information about the flea market fair."

Note to self: Don't piss off Charlotte. "I guess the threat worked."

The store owner snorted. "If the basis is fact, it's not a threat. Bindy emailed the information to me less than thirty minutes later. Like I remembered, amusement rides were added a few years before the fairs stopped happening. The last three, to be exact." She removed a paper from the file with copies of flyers printed on it and laid it on the counter.

Holland peered down at it. Dates were written under them. "Two thousand one, two thousand two and two thousand three."

"Something about one of those years jogged my memory," Charlotte said. "And since I was home, I decided to take a quick look through my records, and I found what I was looking for. The mayor's sister got married in 2002. Since he was the head of the town council, so it was a big to-do. And it made the papers."

Holland sensed something big was coming. She couldn't wait. She had to ask. "Is the blue fabric connected to that wedding?"

"It is. Take a look at this." Charlotte then proceeded to take a photo out of the folder featuring women in a bridal party. They were sitting on a sofa in a brightly lit room with windows. The bridesmaids had on navy blue dresses.

Was the answer to B and L now right in front of her? Holland's legs grew weak.

The names of the women were listed on the photo, but Charlotte didn't need them to point out that the women looked to be in their early twenties, possibly younger. "The bride, Genevieve Ashford Halsey, and maid of honor, Loretta Halsey. Bridesmaids—Callie

Jessep, Tallulah Gordon, Frances Whitehead…and Beryl Franelope Plunkett."

"Wow. That's quite a name." Myles murmured.

Holland pointed to the dark-haired young woman. "So you think Beryl is B in the letters?"

"It adds up. The details in the letter you found. The scrap of fabric that was with it…"

Wanting a better look, Holland picked up the picture. The young girl looked kind of familiar. "Does she still live in town? Is she married?"

"Oh yes. And everyone in Bolan knows who she is, including you. She started using another name when she got married."

As Holland looked into Charlotte's eyes, it was if silent communication was passing between them. Holland spoke up. "Poppy is short for Franelope."

"Wait a minute." Myles pointed. "That's a younger photo of the mayor's *wife*?"

Charlotte nodded. "The B in your letter is Poppy Ashford."

Chapter Eighteen

No one said a word as the revelation hung in the air.

Myles wondered if Holland was thinking the same thing he was—from what he'd learned of small-town life, the mayor's wife possibly cheating on her husband, while they were engaged, could unleash a storm of major proportions.

Holland pointed to the photo and paper with the flyers. "May I have these?"

"Of course." Charlotte put everything back in the folder and handed it to her. "But there's something else you should know. Poppy and the mayor are devoted to each other. Period. And they'll do anything to protect one another. They could care less about the consequences. Also, what she knows, he knows and vice versa." She gave Myles and Holland a pointed look. "So as far as the affair, he already knows about it. Be careful with all this. If I were you, I wouldn't mention it to anyone beyond us until you know exactly what you plan to do with it."

"What about Bindy?" Myles asked. "Won't she tell Anna about the information she sent you and then she'll possibly tell Poppy?"

"Oh no. Not a chance." Charlotte huffed a chuckle. "Poppy views Anna as ridiculous. She would make her sister-in-law's life miserable if she thought that woman knew about the affair. And Anna is so intimidated by her, she'd run from any part of this."

Myles wasn't ready to interpret what all that meant. But it did turn what Charlotte had said earlier completely around. In this situation, the facts could be a threat for the Ashfords—and Holland by default. She didn't know everything, but she had significant proof that helped point to the affair.

Charlotte unlocked the door for them.

Before they walked out, Holland said, "Thank you. Whatever I decide, I won't mention that you or Layla were involved in my search."

Charlotte smiled gratefully. "Thank you. I've sparred enough rounds with Poppy—I'm used it. But Layla and Bastian both hate drama. They wouldn't appreciate being caught in the middle of something."

Myles could definitely relate to the no-drama part. He'd experienced enough of it in his life. And as far as Holland's fake relationship situation, it was far enough away where it wasn't in his face. It was more of an inconvenience than drama.

Outside, the sky had turned dark and cloudy.

The area was almost devoid of pedestrians. The ones that were out hurried toward Brewed Haven, where he'd planned to grab a takeout meal.

Holland looked up as they stood outside the shop. "Good thing we didn't buy those lightning rods. Especially without knowing what they really were."

"That's so true."

Her quiet laugh didn't take away the anxiety he glimpsed on Holland's face before she looked away. Or hide her reluctance to leave.

Right now, she probably needed reassurance or someone as a sounding board. He wanted to be those things for her. He *could* be those things for her. If she let him.

Myles decided to take a shot at what he wanted. "Why don't you come back to the house with me? We'll have dinner and talk about everything."

"I'm driving Chloe's car. I don't want to create any misunderstandings by someone seeing it at your house."

"Leave it here. We'll take mine."

Wind kicked up with a light sprinkling of rain.

Holland didn't answer him or seem overly anxious to get to her car.

He blew out a breath. While he knew he'd promised himself that he wouldn't pressure her to spend time with him, in this particular instance, he felt he should. For both their sakes.

Myles turned toward her. "Holland, you don't need to be alone tonight, and I really want you next to me. Isn't that reason enough for us to break the rules?"

* * *

Moments later, Holland was back in Buttons & Lace Boutique talking to Chloe on the phone.

Charlotte had been surprised to see her walk back in, but Holland needed a few changes of clothes. The older woman had been more than happy to help and was currently in the back storeroom, looking for a pink cardigan in Holland's size.

Holland was good with the decision she'd made with Myles. But it still made her a tad anxious.

Alone in the store, watching the rain fall outside the glass windows, gave her a chance to say the plan out loud. "I'm spending the night with Myles."

"Yay! Your first sleepover at his house. What time am I picking you up?"

"You don't have to pick me up. I'm riding with him. We're downtown. I'm at the boutique buying a few things to tide me over. Myles is picking up carryout at Brewed Haven, so we're all set. But I'm concerned about leaving your car on Main Street overnight. Will it get towed?"

"Don't worry about that. Tristan and I can take care of it."

"I hate to have you drive all the way to town in the rain."

"It's not a problem," Chloe said. "If you were here, I would be taking you to Myles's house and driving back in the rain. There's no difference."

There was *one* major difference. If Holland had been at the guesthouse, she wouldn't be talking to

Chloe at all about a sleepover at Myles's house. By now she would have talked herself out of the plan.

But she was feeling reckless, buying clothes and lacy undergarments she didn't need. After spending the day with Myles, it was too hard to leave him.

He was right. She didn't need to be alone. She also didn't want to be. What she wanted was normal couple's time with Myles. For them to talk about anything and everything until they ran out of words. And she wanted more than just quick sex. Not that it wasn't really good sex, but she also wanted special, intimate moments with him, too.

"Is there anything else I can do?" Chloe asked.

"Just tell me that I'm doing the right thing…" Holland paused. Was she being totally selfish to take a risk like this? She and Nash wouldn't be the only ones who would be collateral damage if this went south.

"Holland…" Reassurance was in Chloe's tone. "It's okay for you to put yourself first. Allow yourself to have this night with Myles."

Holland and Myles walked into the house. Water dripped from the jacket he'd loaned her onto the large black rubber mat in the entryway. They'd gotten drenched running from the driveway to the porch.

Myles set the takeout bag down and took off his boots. His damp shirt clung to his powerful frame.

Holland did the same, setting down her boutique bag and backpack before taking off her boots.

The floor had been repaired, and the faint smell of

new wood was in the air. Beige sconces hung on the walls stripped of wallpaper and gave off a low light.

A lot had happened since she'd last been there. "It's really coming along. And the electricity is working now."

"Actually, it's not. They're still updating some of the wiring in the kitchen and the fuse box. The sconces are battery operated. They were on sale by the dozen at the home improvement store."

"Nice touch, even if they are temporary." Holland slipped off the jacket, and he hung it on a plastic wall hook.

"I figured they were better than a bunch of flashlights. Once the electricity is done, I'll take them down. They've come in handy. I think I'll keep some and donate the rest." He glanced down at her sock-covered feet. "I'm still hammering down a few nails here in there in the floor. I should have mentioned you might want another pair of shoes to walk around in."

"I have them." She searched through the smaller boutique bag, pulled out a pair of beige slip-ons with thick soles and put them on.

Charlotte had suggested the fashionable update to slippers to go with the satin pajamas in the bag. She'd also suggested picking up some sexy lace bikinis. The clothing choices and showing up with Myles had probably tipped the store owner off about the "sleepover."

"I'm glad you picked those up." As he held her waist, he lightly kissed her temple. "I would hate for you to get a splinter."

She rested her hand on his chest. Despite being out in the cold rain, Myles was deliciously warm. Proximity to him and Holland's wet jeans made her shiver.

Myles looked down at her. "You're cold. I'm sorry the fireplace isn't ready yet. But the hot water in the shower will warm you up."

"What about you? Don't you want to get out of those damp clothes?" The memory of how he looked without clothes emerged in her mind and her heart kicked in an extra beat.

From the look on his face, he was having similar thoughts about her. Suddenly she was a lot warmer.

"I will. But you should go first." He kissed her on the forehead then turned to pick up the food bag.

"Or you could join me."

Myles paused. Instead of picking up the bag, his gaze drifted over her from head to toe.

The soft glow of the lights made the need filling his eyes even more intense. "I wouldn't be able to keep my hands off you."

"That's the idea." She went to him and slid her hands up his chest and wound them around his neck.

Myles skimmed his hands up and down the dips in her waist. "And I like that idea a lot…for later." He gave her a long, lingering kiss. "But it's a small shower—there's not enough room for both of us."

"Even better." Holland pressed her lips to his, and they dived back into another heated kiss.

Myles stroking his hands along the outer curves of her breasts and down her waist made her shiver again. He cupped her butt and squeezed, pressing himself against her lower abdomen.

The evidence of how much he wanted her was thrilling and amped up her own need.

His soft groan rumbled into her as he lifted his mouth away. "You're making this so hard."

"That's the point."

She grinned up at him, and he chuckled. "You really are trouble tonight."

"The best kind."

"Yes." He took one of her hands down from around his neck and kissed the back of it. "But for once, we don't have to rush because a contractor is coming or you have to leave. I want to enjoy every minute of tonight with you."

"Allow yourself to have this night with Myles."

That's what Chloe had said earlier. And he was right—they didn't have to rush straight upstairs for once and speed things along. Slowing it down was part of that intimacy she craved. The ease of a slow pace that came with trust and closeness and knowing you could hold on to those minutes he had mentioned. At least for a little while.

"Okay." Holland pressed a quick kiss to his lips before stepping away. "Are there towels upstairs?"

"Yes. In the laundry basket in the middle bedroom."

He took the food to the kitchen, and she carried her things to the bedroom.

After a nice hot shower, she returned to the bedroom across the hall, wrapped in a towel, and changed into the bikinis and button-down top of her new satin pj's.

Excitement and a little anxiety bubbled inside her. Even though they'd already slept together, tonight felt extra special. That this was the first time of something thrilling and new. A next step in their relationship.

Outside the half-closed door, she heard Myles walking down the hall. He called out, "I'm taking a quick shower. If you're hungry, go ahead and eat. I'll be done in a few minutes."

"Okay." But she wasn't in a hurry. They could eat together.

Holland took a zippered pouch from her bag. Rina had given it to Myles at Brewed Haven when he'd gotten the food.

Apparently, Chloe had made a call to Rina. It contained lip gloss, body butter and other handy toiletries, along with a silk pillowcase so she wouldn't damage her hair while she slept.

It was so thoughtful of Chloe and Rina. And Chloe wouldn't have reached out to Rina unless she trusted her to keep Myles and Holland's secret.

Holland took her time moisturizing her hair. Then she took out the body butter. She should have put this on after she'd gotten out the shower.

Propping her leg on the edge of the bed, she massaged cream onto her skin. The light fragrance was a mix of shea butter, vanilla and coconut. She would definitely buy more in the future. Holland opened the buttons of her shirt to put more on.

Myles came into the bedroom, wearing a towel around his waist. "Did you see…"

His voice trailed away as he stared at her.

The way his gaze took in Holland was like a caress. It emboldened her to turn and give him a clearer view.

His chest rose and fell with a ragged breath. The evidence of his desire stirred beneath the towel.

Holland slowly slipped the shirt from her shoulders. She let it slide down her arms to the floor, leaving her wearing only the bikinis.

He walked toward her as if he was in a trance.

Myles reached for her, but she stepped out of reach. She dropped her gaze to where the towel was tucked at his waist, then looked back to his eyes.

Message received, he unfastened the towel and let it drop.

Reaching out, she glided her hands over his abs and pecs. His torso had become even more defined from the hard work he was putting into remodeling the house.

She glided her hands downward, and the angles of his jawline became more defined along with the dips and valleys in his abdomen.

Tension emanated from him. He was clearly keeping himself reined in, allowing her to touch him as she pleased. The hit-and-run intimate moments they'd been sharing hadn't allowed time for this. They'd been like tiny sips of champagne, a teasing prelude to goodness. But being here with him now was like finally being able to get her hands on a full bottle.

But that didn't mean there shouldn't be any teasing at all.

Stepping closer, she brushed a barely there kiss over his lips, and then another. He chased her mouth, but she leaned away. She pressed a slightly harder kiss to his mouth, and as his tongue glided across her lips, she let him in for a small taste before leaning away again.

He stilled. Under his watchful gaze, Holland knew she was playing with fire. The tips of her breasts tingled from brushing against his chest, desire pooling like warmed honey in her middle. She ached for him so much it physically hurt. But, at the same time, the thrill of slowing the moment and seeing and feeling how much he wanted her was like an aphrodisiac.

She moved her hand lower, stopping just shy of his erection. Holland glided her hand back up and then down again.

"Holland…" The way he whispered her name was her only warning before he caught her hand, moved it aside and brought her against him.

He kissed her hard and deep. Myles backed her down onto the mattress and soon she was lost in slow caresses that ignited desire. She arched up for more of them and quickly discovered that rushing wasn't part of his plan.

The warmth of his mouth as he sucked the peaks of her breasts. The brush of his lips down her belly. The way he fit his hands to her curves as he trailed heated, open-mouthed kisses over her skin brought Holland to a place of pure erotic sensation.

Long moments later, as he moved down even lower between her legs, she gripped his shoulders. The pleasure was so intense, she warred between wanting more or begging him to stop. She cried out his name.

As she floated in the afterglow of her orgasm, Myles briefly left her to put on a condom. They stared into each other's eyes as he glided into her.

He pleased her. Worshipped her. When she reached her climax, what she felt, what was true was unmistakable. He was the one she wanted. Now…and in the future.

Chapter Nineteen

The next morning, Myles pried one eye open. He saw sunlight, and Holland sitting on the bed wearing her pajama top, poised to take a picture with her camera.

He groaned. "Holland, it's too early for that." Putting up a hand, he blocked his face just as the shutter clicked.

"Nooo!" She feigned a pout. "It was the perfect picture and you ruined it."

"How can a picture of me just waking up be perfect?"

She glanced around. "The light in this room is so incredible, it's practically impossible to take a bad one."

"Let me see. Give me the camera." He sat up against the pillow.

Holland handed him the Nikon. As he pointed the

lens at her, she looked away and struck a model-like pose sitting on the bed.

She was right. It was impossible to take a bad photo of her, but it had more to do with Holland than the sunlight filling the room.

Hints of auburn gleamed in her hair. Every inch of her face, along with the rest of her, looked radiant, smooth and flawless.

Myles set the camera aside and held his arms open. "Come here. Let me hold you."

Holland snuggled to his side and laid her head on his chest. She fit perfectly against him.

Yesterday at the bazaar. Being together last night. Waking up to see her face this morning. This was what he wanted to do with her. To just be a normal couple,.

But because of someone else's choices, they couldn't.

No. He wouldn't think about that now. Instead, he would focus on the here and now. Soon they would have to remain at arm's length again.

Myles stroked along her hip. "So what's your plans for the rest of the day?"

Her sigh blew across his skin. "Honestly, after last night's talk with Charlotte, I'm not sure I have plans anymore. Or what they should be."

"You don't want to make the documentary anymore?"

"No, the opposite. I can already see it in my mind. This house in the present day. The fireplace. The letter. The ripped fabric. The unfolding of L and B's love story explained in a reenactment."

"And the ending?"

"That's my problem." She slowly traced a spiral of circles on his chest. "If I tell the truth, there's a problem. If I don't, it could diminish the documentary, and that's not good, either." She sighed. "If I'm not going to tell the story right, should I even tell it at all?"

He intertwined his fingers with hers on his chest. "You could choose another house with another story you *can* tell."

"Is that what you think I should do?" Sadness tinged her voice. "Just change my creative vision?"

Myles hesitated. Maybe he did. Poppy Ashford intimidated people to the point of being afraid to cross her. Or they tried to find ways to lessen the impact of her wrath.

He admired Holland's ability to want to see the story clearly. But he also worried that she wasn't approaching this with a healthy dose of caution. So any way he looked at it, this was an impossible situation. Because dampening her vision wouldn't be just a compromise. It could make her less of who she was as an artist.

"I think you should weigh all sides and do what feels right," Myles finally said.

Holland sat up and tucked her legs under her. "A part of me wants to approach Poppy with the letter and see what she says. I mean, what could it hurt?

She and the mayor are happily married with a family now."

"And because of that you think she'll be okay with you doing what will basically be an exposé about her love life and an affair?"

"That's just it. That's not the important part." She sat up straighter as conviction came into her voice. "It's much bigger than that. It's a timeless story about choices. Making them. Living with them. How other people's choices can impact ours and the trajectory of our lives. I'm interested in knowing why she made hers."

But the thing about choices, the motives weren't always clear or easy to define, especially in hindsight. As often as Myles had mulled over the decisions he and Sydney had made, he couldn't always pinpoint the reason for them.

Holland would have to be prepared for possibly not discovering answers. Just more questions.

"You said a *part* of you wants to do that. What about the rest?"

"I don't know." Holland breathed out a single wry chuckle. "Stay here with you today and not think about it."

Myles reached out and took her hand. "That's your choice." He grinned. "You know what my answer is to that."

Indecision flashed in her eyes even as she returned his smile. Holland curled back up against him.

He'd heard something once about writers writing the story they need to read because it spoke to them in some way. And because of that, only the writer knew the full story. As a storyteller, was Poppy's story the one Holland needed to hear and see? Was her fixation with the story really about her own choices?

Myles wrapped both arms around Holland and held her a bit tighter. If it was, even knowing Holland for a short time, he sensed making that suggestion to her wouldn't go over well. She would need to find that out on her own for it to resonate. But at what cost?

Holland spent the day with Myles. And he put her to work, having her help him install cabinetry in the kitchen and bathrooms and painting walls. The walnut-cream color of paint was perfect for the living and dining room spaces.

Later that night, as the house aired out, they sat on the air mattress he'd placed directly in front of the back deck, eating pepperoni pizza.

The tree branches swayed and rustled in a slow breeze that had less of a chill behind it and more of the warmth of spring preparing for summer.

She was happily exhausted.

Myles came out the house carrying a can of soda and a bottle of beer.

The light beige paint spattered on his white T-shirt and jeans was the same color on the worn blue T-shirt she'd borrowed from him.

He handed her the soda and sat with her.

Holland waited for him and the mattress to settle

before opening the can. As she took a long sip, carbonated bubbles danced across her tongue. She set the can on the ground.

Myles was smiling at her in a way that she couldn't help but smile back at him.

She'd caught him staring at her several times throughout the day. When she'd asked him about it, he'd said there was no particular reason.

Or maybe there was a reason this time. What was that dripping down her chin? She swiped over the spot. Pepperoni grease.

Chuckling, Myles handed her a napkin. "You also have tomato sauce on your cheek."

"I do?" She wiped where he pointed. "Did I get it?"

"Yeah. You're good."

"Why didn't you tell me I had food on my face?"

He shrugged. "I don't care. You're still cute to me."

"Oh, so you like me because I wear food well?"

"Well…" Myles stroked his chin and mocked deep contemplation.

He liked her with food on her face. She liked the faint stubble on his jawline. He looked even sexier.

He continued, "Okay. Food on your face. Definitely not top of the list. The way you wiggle your hips when you climb a ladder. That's at the top."

"So that's why you were always behind me when I was on the ladder."

"I was making sure you didn't fall and hurt yourself."

"From less than two feet off the ground?"

Humor brimmed in his eyes. "I was being cautious." His smile sobered. "I'm glad you stayed."

"I am, too. I never knew tools could be so fun. And now I know how to install cabinets."

He was staring at her again. But this time he had a contemplative expression.

"What are you thinking? And don't say nothing, because it's not true."

"I wish I didn't have pepperoni breath so I could kiss you."

"We actually can kiss. You and I are twinsies. We've both got pepperoni breath *and paint covered* shirts that match."

Myles gave her peck on the mouth. Smiling, he leaned away. "But only one of us has pepperoni and beer breath. I'll wait until after I brush my teeth to give you a real kiss. But there is something I wanted to ask you." He pointed between the two of them. "How do you feel about me and you doing more of this after we leave Bolan?"

Happiness leaped inside her. "Yes. I mean, yes, I'm in. Long-distance relationships can be hard at times, but they also can work. Especially if we're willing to do what it takes."

The smile on his face sobered a little as seriousness crept into his eyes. "It is a big step." He stood. "We should get cleaned up, sit down and really talk about it inside."

"Okay." Holland reached up and too his hand as he helped her off the mattress

Maybe she shouldn't have mentioned the hard

parts of a long-distance relationship so soon and just told him she was excited about continuing their relationship. That's honestly how she felt. She'd make that clear to him when they talked inside.

He took her hand and led her toward the door. "I'll clean up out here while you take a shower."

"Okay." She had more sexy bikinis he hadn't seen yet. Holland saw a celebration ahead—after their talk.

Just past the door, he let go of her hand and snatched the hammer from the toolbox on the floor. "Lock the doors behind me."

"What…but aren't you coming back inside?"

A yelp and rustling tree limbs followed by a hard thump came from across the lawn. "Get inside," Myles yelled as he sprinted in that direction.

Alarm momentarily froze Holland in place. Heart knocking against her rib cage, she closed the French doors and turned the lock. Peering through the glass, she searched for Myles.

Was he okay? Who was out there? Or was it an animal of some kind? Her imagination went into overdrive with images of wolves or bears.

Myles stalked out of the trees and toward the house.

She rushed out to meet him. "What was it? What happened?"

He hustled her back inside. "Someone was out there. But I lost them in the dark." Tension hummed through him, and irritation filled his face. "I heard a car speed off. They're lucky they got away."

"*Lucky?* What were you thinking, running into the woods like that? You...you could have gotten hurt." Reality ballooned in her chest, making it harder to breathe. She whacked his arm.

"I'm sorry." Myles dropped the hammer in the toolbox. He embraced her, and she buried her face into his chest. "You're shaking." He sounded surprised. "Hey, I'm okay. I didn't mean to scare you."

Holland wrapped her arms around him. "Well, you did."

"I'm sorry." He released a heavy breath. "It just ticked me off that someone was spying on us."

"Spying? You think that's what they were doing."

"They climbed into a tree and hid. While we were sitting out there, I thought I caught a flash out the corner of my eye."

Panic flowed through her. "You mean like a camera flash?"

"Maybe. I don't know." Myles went to the kitchen counter and picked up his phone.

"Who are you calling?"

"The police. They need to know about this. Whoever it was might still be in the area."

"You...you should call them." Holland swallowed hard. She'd almost said, "you can't." But he was right. The police should be alerted so they could investigate. And she needed to get out of there. "It won't take me long to grab my things." She turned toward the stairs. "And where are your keys? I have to take your car since mine isn't here."

"My car keys?" He caught her hand. "You're not leaving."

"I can't be here when the police arrive."

Confusion came and went from his eyes. Anger replaced it. He let go of her. "Nash… You're not supposed to be here with me because of him."

"It's not just about him. There's a lot more at stake. You know that."

Myles pointed to the backyard. "All I know is some unknown trespasser who possibly wanted to cause you harm was out there." His voice grew louder. "Actually, they could still be out there somewhere, and maybe they're not alone. And all you can think about is covering Nash's ass? What *I* am thinking about right now…" He looked directly into her eyes. "Is you and only you. I need you safe because I care about you, Holland. And if that means calling the police and exposing that you were here to the world, so be it."

The intensity of his words and the concern mixed with caring in his gaze melted everything else away. "I care about you, too." She allowed him to tug her back to him.

Myles wrapped an arm around her, cupped her cheek and laid his forehead to hers.

Their rushed breathing slowed and synced.

"I shouldn't have yelled at you," he rasped. "I'm sorry."

"I'm sorry, too." She laid her hands on his chest.

His heart beat solidly against her palm. "You're right. I shouldn't be fighting with you."

Myles leaned away from her. He took a deeper breath. "I know who to call."

Chapter Twenty

Thirty minutes later, Mace Calderone stood in the living room. Myles had called Tristan, and he'd tracked the deputy sheriff down. Luckily, he was working that night.

Mace turned down the volume on the radio clipped to his tactical belt. The tan shirt of his uniform shaped against his bulletproof vest underneath. "Whoever was out there is long gone. With just flashlights, it's hard to see anything. I'll stop back by near the end of my shift. The sun will be up by then, and it'll be easier to see what might have been going on back there. If they fell out of the tree like you mentioned, they may have dropped something that could identify them."

The memory of Myles sprinting across the backyard into potential danger came into Holland's mind.

He'd mentioned worrying about her safety. What about his? She leaned more heavily against him, grateful that nothing terrible had happened while he'd tried to chase down the intruder who'd been in the trees.

"I hope so, because I want you to catch them. We both do." Myles rubbed his hand up and down her back as he addressed the deputy. "We appreciate you coming out here to personally take the report."

"I understand the need for privacy." Mace's gaze momentarily shifted to Holland. "We can't rule out that this perpetrator could be a member of the press trying to get a lead on a story. Or even a stalker or an ex-boyfriend." He cleared his throat. "Holland, have there been any suspicious individuals hanging around you since you've been here or in California? Or has anything happened that could be perceived as a threat?"

Myles tensed, and his hand stalled at her waist.

Holland glanced up at him. He couldn't be thinking what she thought he was.

Mace's direct gaze moved between Holland and Myles. "If there is something going on, I need to know."

It was too late to deny it. "Yes" was practically stamped on Myles's furrowed brow.

But it couldn't be this. "Remember we mentioned finding a letter in the fireplace here?" Holland murmured. "Well, I might know who B is."

Mace raised a brow, waiting for her to continue.

"I don't know who the man was, but I believe the

woman he was writing to was Poppy Ashford. Her first name is Beryl. But as you know, she goes by Poppy. There's a good chance her sister-in-law Anna may know what I've found out and told her."

Mace's brow raised a fraction more. "So you're saying Poppy cheated on the mayor while they were engaged?" He released a low whistle. "Yeah, that's something the Ashfords wouldn't want to get out. Especially since he's thinking about running for senator."

"Exactly," Myles interjected. "You never know what people will do when they feel threatened. And from Poppy's perspective, her past coming back to haunt her could be a significant threat for her."

"True. And Poppy and the mayor are protective of each other." Mace's expression turned skeptical. "But I can't see either of them hiding out in a tree. Poppy operates like a blunt instrument. She'll threaten you face-to-face. And the mayor, he's the negotiator type. He's more likely to offer you a check to forget the whole thing. One of your wild cards is the guy who wrote the letter. If he's still around, he could have more to lose."

Myles released a harsh breath. "I don't like that scenario one bit. The quickest way to find out who the guy is would be for us to ask Poppy."

"Which I don't advise," Mace warned. "Holland said Poppy *might* be the woman in the letter. Making untrue accusations could get you into legal trouble. The other wild card you have to consider are the teens who were vandalizing your property. The two of you were outside on a bed."

"No, you've got the wrong idea," she protested. "We were using it as a couch and a table. We weren't fooling around."

The deputy sheriff waved her off. "I'm not judging, just saying. If teenagers were out there and thought you two were about to get busy, they may have climbed a tree to get a better look. We have to consider all the options."

Myles gave Holland's waist a squeeze as he looked at Mace. "We understand. What's the next step?"

"Once I file this report, the department will be on the lookout for trespassers in general. In the meantime, just stay alert. If anything looks or feels suspicious, call me. If I need to ask more questions, will I be able to find both of you here?"

Myles spoke up first. "I have a meeting in New Jersey in the morning, but I'll be back tomorrow night."

Holland responded, "I'll be at the guesthouse."

Mace looked at her. "You might want to hold off on researching anything connected to the letter for little while, just in case."

After letting the deputy sheriff out, Myles stayed by the door. "Maybe you should come with me tomorrow."

"I appreciate the offer. But you have a client meeting to focus on. I would feel like I was getting in the way."

He came over to her. "So if you're not coming with me, what's your plan for tomorrow?"

"I've got scripts waiting in my inbox. It feels like my vacation is over, so I might get started on them. Or if I hear of anything interesting about a house, I might go see it."

"Do me a favor?" As she nodded, he brought her into a loose embrace. "Don't visit any houses alone while I'm gone, and steer clear of any letter research like Mace suggested?"

The worry on his face got to her. This wasn't how it was supposed to be. Holland wrapped her arms tightly around his waist. "I promise, I'll be safe. Everything's going to be fine."

But even as Holland said it, she could hear the sliver of doubt in her tone. She couldn't help but wonder who'd been lurking in the trees. And what they'd been up to.

The next day, Myles ended the presentation on his laptop that appeared on the flat screen on the wall in the sleek, modern conference room. Adjusting his position in the padded chair, he smoothed his burgundy tie.

After wearing casual clothes and boots for the past few weeks, it had taken a minute to adjust to his navy business suit and Testoni lace-ups image.

But once he'd arrived in New Jersey, his focus had been on the three Odom Construction executives sitting across from him at the table. At least it had been most of the time.

Before the meeting started, his mind had wandered to earlier that morning when he'd dropped Holland off at the guesthouse. The sun was just creeping over the horizon, but even in the semidarkness he could see she hadn't slept well. Neither had he. They'd both been up, but instead of talking, they'd just held each other all night.

Maybe they should have started the discussion about being in a long-distance relationship and what that might mean for them. But he did want to run an idea by her. She could use his house as a home base as she continued to research and develop her documentary. That way, she could come to Bolan whenever she needed. She wouldn't have to use the guesthouse. Holland would have a home. And he would come home to her whenever he could get away.

It wasn't a far leap in his mind to see it. During the times they'd shared at the house, being there with her had felt so natural. He wasn't rushing anything. But thinking about how things might move forward for them made him…happy.

Warmth expanded in Myles's chest.

Lowell Odom, a fit-looking older man with neatly clipped gray hair, leaned in. "So your software will allow us to see where we're making or losing money in real time?"

Myles pulled his thoughts away from Holland.

"Yes. Knowing where you stand at any given moment allows you to make the course corrections you need at that time, not weeks or months later when you've lost critical resources."

Lowell's daughter, a dark-haired woman who'd inherited his slightly bulbous nose, asked, "What about integration and training?"

"Integration is usually a smooth process, particularly on the financial end. But as a whole, a smooth transition depends on if your current monitoring platforms, systems and equipment are up to date."

Myles went on to explain how training would work.

From the expressions of Lowell, his daughter and the third executive, they were pleased with what they'd heard from him.

A short time later, it was just Lowell and Myles getting on the elevator. Lowell was meeting his son and grandchildren for lunch.

As the elevator glided down from the fourth floor to the lobby, the older man said, "You have a few calluses on your palms like I do. Mine come from crewing. I'm on the lake in back of our house five days a week. What about yours?"

"I'm remodeling a house in Maryland. I have to admit, I hadn't planned on doing it, but it's working out well for me."

Lowell nodded knowingly. "In my opinion, doing good, solid work with your hands keeps a person on track about life and priorities. That and a solid family life."

Myles had a good feeling about winning this contract. It was always a great sign when the owner of a company continued the dialogue after a presentation.

They walked across the lobby together and out the front door.

Myles turned to shake Lowell's hand again and thank him for his time.

A young guy with dark, messy hair and a sly grin stuck a camera in front of Myles's face and snapped a photo.

"Hey!" On a reflex, Myles pushed aside the camera. "Get that away from me."

Lowell took a defensive stance. "Leave, or I'm calling the police."

"No need to get your boxers in a bunch, old man. I got what I needed." The obnoxious guy grinned wider. "But I do have a question for Myles. What's it like banging Nash Moreland's fiancée?"

Chapter Twenty-One

Holland sat tailor-style with her legs up under her, reading scripts she might want to acquire.

The best one so far was a remake of the classic comedy *Father of the Bride*. But instead of the father having all the feels about his young daughter getting married, this script was focused on the mom whose son was marrying her former best friend.

Holland glanced at the phone on the coffee table, checking the time. It was almost noon. Myles had said he would call and let her know how his meeting had gone that morning. She hadn't heard from him yet. Maybe the meeting had rolled into lunch. That was always a good sign. Or perhaps he was already on his way back, possibly planning to surprise her.

Things had been a little somber between them this morning. But their goodbye kiss had been perfect and sweet with the promise of missing each other. Tonight's reunion would be equally as wonderful. She'd arranged for Dominic Crawford to prepare a sumptuous takeaway meal of buttered whiskey steak and shaved brussels sprouts. And they were having Rina's peach pie for dessert. She was also borrowing a four-top dining table and chairs from Pasture Lane.

Tonight would be the perfect time for them to talk about their future.

A knock sounded at the door. Holland set her computer aside, sprang to her feet and opened the it.

She blinked. Trying to reconcile why blond-haired, blue-eyed Nash Moreland was at her door.

Before she could ask, he strolled in and glanced around. "Nice place. Is anyone here with you?"

"No. And why are you here?"

"Hold on a sec." He tapped out a text on his phone.

A beat or two later, her phone rang on the coffee table. She answered the video call, and Burke's face appeared on screen. He was in the back of his Range Rover. "Burke, what's going on? Why is Nash here?"

Burke spoke calmly and slowly. "First, I need you to take a deep breath. And next, I need you to trust that everything Nash is about to help you do and what we're about to do from now on is best for everyone. It's not going to feel like it, but it is."

"No." The heat of frustration and disbelief burned through her. "I will not get engaged to Nash. I'm done! End of conversation."

"Ouch." Nash feigned a wince. "Being engaged to me wouldn't be *that* bad."

"No." Burke shook his head. "That's not it. Nash," he called out. "Show her."

Her ex held out his phone so Holland could see the screen. It was a picture of her and Myles on the air mattress in his backyard. The photographer had captured the exact moment he'd pecked her on the lips. Instead of a low-key, greasy-pizza moment, it looked like they were swept up in the throes of passion.

The pancakes she'd eaten as a late breakfast swirled in her stomach. "No…"

As Nash flipped over to a video, icy dread consumed her. Someone had filmed Myles dressed in a business suit, walking out of a building with an older man. A photographer put a camera in his face, and Myles pushed it away. Words were exchanged that she couldn't make out, but one part came in clearly.

"I do have a question for Myles. What's it like banging Nash Moreland's fiancée?"

Nausea roiled through her. Holland tossed her phone on the couch and ran to the toilet in the bathroom. Despair came out with the purge.

Nash pressed a cold washcloth to her nape.

When she was done, she used it to wipe her face.

Nash gave her privacy as she went to the bathroom in the main bedroom to wash her face and the bitter taste from her mouth.

She walked into the bedroom.

Nash stood in the doorway with his hands resting on either side of the frame. "Are you okay?"

His nonchalant concern and *I've got this handled* attitude had always annoyed her. Whenever there was a problem, it seemed liked he actually believed a hanging cable would appear out of nowhere, he'd take hold of it, wrap an arm around her and swing them into a helicopter waiting to whisk them off to a place where the problem no longer existed.

Funny thing was, she almost wished that could happen now. And that helicopter would take her to Myles.

Dread rushed through her. Where was he? What was he thinking? He must hate her.

She tried to push past Nash, but he blocked her way. "I need to call Myles."

"You can't." As he looked at her, genuine concern came into his blue eyes. "You and I are getting on a plane and flying back to LA in about four hours. Once we get back home, our publicists will do their magic. The plan is to put out a joint statement that you didn't cheat on me. We were on a break, but now we're back together. They've also started lining up events for us to attend together."

"No. This isn't about saving your image anymore. This is about me and Myles. I care about him."

Nash gave her an exasperated look. "We're not doing this for me. We're doing this for *him*. Right now, if he's not dealing with the same tag-team maneuver he just went through in New Jersey to get a reaction out of him, he's fielding hate messages from my millions of followers on social media. And he's probably gotten a few nasty emails and phone calls as well. Announcing that we were on a break, and you weren't cheating on me with him, takes some of that pressure off."

"No." She shook her head. "That's not the only way."

"It's the best way, and you know that. He'll probably have to change his phone number and not go on his socials for a while, but the more we solidify our relationship, the faster the celebrity news cycle takes its focus off him." Nash gave her an empathetic look. One of the most genuine expressions she'd ever seen on his face. "You have to remember, we're used to this type of bullshit. Myles isn't. I know it's hard to face, but the best thing you could do for him might be to walk away and just let him get his life back to normal."

Her phone rang in her living room. She recognized the chime.

"It's Myles. I have to talk to him." Holland shoved Nash, and somehow she managed to move him aside.

Running to the phone, she snatched it from the couch on the fourth ring. "Myles, are you okay? Are you at the house?"

"No." He sounded tired. "Tristan called and said not to come back to Bolan yet. People are snooping around and asking questions about you, me and Nash. I'm in New York, at my brother's place."

Of course he couldn't come back to Maryland yet. What was she thinking? Everything there was a mess. And it was because of her. He didn't deserve any of this.

The remembered image of his face on the video—

angry, maybe even a little confused—brought tears to her eyes. She sat down on the couch. "I saw the video of the photographer hounding you in New Jersey. I'm so sorry that happened to you. You have every right to be irritated with me."

"I'm not irritated with you, Holland. I'm irritated about the situation. What about you? How are you holding up?"

"I hate this type of attention," she admitted. "It's an inconvenience, but I've learned to roll with it."

"Roll with it." He released a harsh laugh. "I don't even see how that's possible. Those vultures, those so-called photographers and reporters, just don't care. I missed out on a contract worth millions because of them."

"Oh no, they saw the video?"

"The owner of the company was in the video. He was with me when I got ambushed."

She recalled that in the video, there had been an older man with Myles. She'd thought it was some passerby. "Myles, what can I do?"

"About the contract? Nothing." He released a long breath. "Can you come to New York? My brother's building has a doorman. Once you're inside, no one will bother us. We should be okay."

Holland closed her eyes, imagining herself flying to New York, getting off the plane and seeing Myles waiting for her. She wanted that so much. "I wish I could come to you right now. But I can't. I have to go back to LA."

"For how long?"

Nash walked from the main bedroom into the kitchen.

It took a second for her brain to register his presence. She's been so concerned about Myles she'd blocked her ex-boyfriend out.

"I don't know. We have to…"

What? Manage the fallout to save Nash's image? Work to solve the problem of the first lie that was created? The cost for Myles had been immediate.

Nash set up the Keurig. His every movement, from finding a mug to locating teaspoons to pouring water, reverberated.

She shot him a look, and Nash ignored her, going about his business of making coffee.

She got up, walked back into the main bedroom and shut the door. "I'll know more about what's happening once I get there and we have a few meetings."

The door opened. "Holl—" Nash used the nickname he'd given her years ago. He knew she hated it. "I'm making coffee. Do you want some? And where's the sugar?"

"Who's with you?" Myles asked.

Caught between questions, she shook her head at Nash and answered Myles. "Burke sent someone to escort me. It's just a precaution."

"A bodyguard?"

"No, not a bodyguard…"

Standing in the doorway, Nash crossed his arms over his chest and leaned on one side of the doorjamb. He stared at Holland as if daring her to tell Myles the truth.

Myles spoke. "He's there, isn't he? Nash. Why the hell is he there with you?."

"It's…not what you think. He's just here because we have to figure out how to handle the situation."

"Our situation? Or the situation with you and Nash?"

Holland couldn't stop herself from looking to Nash as she remembered his words from earlier.

"You have to remember, we're used to this type of bullshit. Myles isn't."

No. Myles would understand. She just had to explain it to him. "I need to see you. Can we please switch to video?"

His long exhale echoed. "Sure."

She motioned for Nash to leave, and he reluctantly walked away.

Holland tapped the video request on her phone, Myles accepted it and, a moment later, his face appeared on the screen.

She released an exhale of relief. He looked wonderful to her but also stressed out.

Myles's steady gaze connected with hers. "So what were you saying about Nash?"

She hadn't been talking about Nash. He had. But now wasn't the time to correct him. "A statement is being made that Nash and I were on a break while I was here. So you and me being together wasn't cheating."

Myles shook his head. "Why not just clear it up by saying you weren't with Nash in the first place? That we are together."

"That would make him look like a liar and possibly take us right back where we started with the Gina situation."

"What about *our* situation?"

Uncertainty churned inside of her as she struggled to find the right words to explain it to him. "The faster the celebrity news cycle takes its focus off you, the faster your life can get back to normal."

"When that happens, where will you be? Pretending to be with Nash or really being with me."

"I'm with you, Myles. Even when I'm with him." *Wait. No!* That didn't sound right.

He looked down for a long moment, then back at her. Misery reflected on his face. "Pretending and playing games with the truth. Yes, I did it with Sydney, but we had a plan. It wasn't going to be forever. With you, it just seems to be the standard. I want to be with you, but I can't do it this way."

Guilt squeezed around her heart. He was unhappy because she was making him that way.

"The best thing you could do for him might be to walk away and just let him get his life back to normal..."

As Holland opened her mouth to speak, tears rolled down her cheeks. She wanted to plead with Myles. To beg him to wait it out. But that was selfish.

She didn't want to let go of what they had. She wanted a second chance to make everything right.

But she also wanted the best for him. For Myles to be truly happy. And he wouldn't find that if they stayed together.

Holland dried her cheeks. She wasn't an actress, but she was about to deliver the most convincing line she'd ever said, no matter how much it hurt. "You're right." She swallowed against the tightness in her throat. "What's going on now is my life 24-7. And I like it that way. So...instead of trying to go forward, we need to end it now."

"What? Wait, Holland, you don't mean that."

The shock and confusion registering on Myles's face was like a punch that almost made Holland double over with emotional pain.

Lifting her chin, she forced herself to look at him on the screen. "Yes. I do."

Hurt shown in his eyes. He swallowed and his jawline angled and ticked. As his gaze hardened, frustration and resignation reflected on his face. "Fine, if that's what you want."

. Holland fought with the part of her that screamed out. *No! It isn't. I love you, Myles. I love you...*

The ending of the call was a blur of white noise in her head. A moment later, Myles was gone from the screen. She stared still trying to process what had happened, what she'd lost while her heart tried to thump with the weight of pain. It was over.

She walked out of the bedroom.

Nash was sitting on the couch. He'd heard it all, from the rare look of empathy on his face. He stood. "I'm sorry."

As the tears fell, she let Nash hold her and tell her she was going to be all right. But he was the wrong man. She didn't want him. Holland wanted Myles.

Chapter Twenty-Two

Holland haphazardly tossed her clothes into the suitcase on the bed. Her eyes were swollen, and despite all the tears that had poured out, they still felt full. Saying goodbye to Myles was the hardest thing she'd ever done. But it was also the right thing, wasn't it? Their lives just didn't fit together. Now Myles could find someone that did fit with his.

Her phone rang on the bed. She didn't recognize the number. Maybe it was Myles. Had he gotten a temporary phone because he was being harassed on his real one? Or was that someone calling to harass *her*? So far her private number had remained confidential, but her social media messages were blowing up. And the few comments she'd read on posts about her and Myles were vile, mean and twisted. People just assumed they knew the truth.

Holland had also looked at Myles's Facebook time-line. Someone claiming he was an opportunist and a leech was the nicest comment there. She'd wanted to respond and tell them he was none of those horrible things.

Myles was strong, hardworking, loyal, reliable, and caring.

A moment later, a voice mail alert dinged.

Curious, she listened to it.

"Hello, Holland. It's Poppy Ashford."

The air of superiority in the woman's voice almost made her hang up.

"I heard what's going on, and it's just awful. I understand you're leaving later today. But I hope you can spare me a minute of your time. We really need to talk."

The message ended, and Holland released a derisive snort as she slipped the phone into the side pocket of her green cargo pants. Talk? She pushed up the sleeves of her white midriff sweater. Poppy clearly wanted to discuss the letter and maybe threaten her over what she'd found out.

Right now, she could care less about what the mayor's wife had done over two decades ago or whom she'd done it with. Everyone was right about the woman—she really didn't have an empathetic bone in her body—because if Poppy had, she wouldn't have intruded on the worst day of Holland's life asking her to spare anything, especially her time.

"Hey, Holland." Nash knocked on the bedroom doorjamb. "It looks like the car that's taking us to the airport will be here in twenty minutes. They're really early. Do you want to leave when it gets here, or should I tell the driver to wait until you're ready to go?"

Why prolong the misery? And from what she'd heard, Tillbridge Horse Stable and Guesthouse had to beef up security. Once the press heard Nash was there, they'd started flocking in from the surrounding area. Now Chloe, Dominic and Philippa would be affected as well.

Her friends enjoyed relative anonymity in Bolan, and now she was screwing up their peaceful lives, too. As long as she was in Bolan, her presence would continue to make the people she cared about miserable.

Holland walked out and stuffed her makeup bag into her backpack. "I'll be ready. We can leave as soon as they get here."

When the chauffeured town car arrived, Holland and Nash were hustled out of the guesthouse through the staffless kitchen to the loading dock, where it was parked.

As soon as she and Nash settled in the back, the driver sped off.

The countryside she'd come to know well in the last few weeks flew past the dark, tinted windows.

Chloe's car…she still had the keys. *Damn...* She'd have to mail them to her.

Nash raised the privacy glass between them and the driver. "Burke sent me a text. His private plane is already on the tarmac. They're adjusting our departure time. We won't have to wait. Oh, and the crew is asking for our meal preferences—steak, chicken or fish—and if we have any special requests."

The thought of food made Holland ill. "I don't care. You pick everything."

"Chicken for both of us, then. Fish will stink up the plane. I really need some Fiji Water and grapes. Wait, I can't." He frowned. "I have a photo shoot in a couple of weeks, so I have to rough it. No carbs. Otherwise my abs won't show up in the photos."

Rolling her eyes at his theatrics, Holland looked out the window. The Ashfords' home, high on the hill, came into view.

Maybe Poppy didn't want to threaten her. Maybe the mayor's wife wanted to gloat. The timing of Charlotte giving her the information about Poppy and a photographer hiding in the trees a couple days later was conspicuous. What could Poppy want to tell her?

Reaching forward, she pressed the button that lowered the privacy glass. "Pull into the driveway on the left, please."

"Yes, ma'am," the driver responded.

Nash looked bewildered. "Why are we stopping here? Whose house is this?"

"I have business to take care of. Just stay in the car."

"Burke told me not to let you out of my sight."

That sounded like what he'd say. "Nash, I'm not making a run for it. I just need to clear the air with someone before I leave. It won't take long."

The car reached the security station, and the driver gave the guard Holland's name. Moments later, the guard let them pass.

When the driver parked in front of the three-story house with pillars on the front porch, Holland immediately got out, walked up the steps and rang the doorbell.

Moments later, a neatly dressed brunette opened the door. "Hello, Ms. Ainsley. My name is Nara. I'm Mrs. Ashford's assistant. Come in. She's waiting for you."

She followed the woman down a red-carpeted corridor. The bottom floor was impressive and stately, tastefully decorated with Queen Anne furniture and blush-colored ceiling-to-floor drapes bordering the windows.

They stopped at a room on the right.

Poppy sat on a vintage-looking sofa with dark wood trim. Her attire of brown slacks and a soft-looking tan pullover sweater was simple yet elegant. She'd enhanced the outfit with delicate gold jewelry. Her straight blond hair brushed along her shoulders.

Her bearing said everything. This was her house, and she was the undisputed queen. "Holland, I'm so glad you could stop by." Poppy's smile barely lifted her cheeks as she gestured politely to a side chair. "Please have a seat. I'm having lemonade. Would you like some? If not, Nara can bring you something else."

"No, thank you." Holland took a seat. The way the chair was designed, she could either sink back awkwardly or perch near the edge of the cushion. She chose the latter.

Poppy picked up her tall glass of lemonade from the oval coffee table. She took a sip, then set it back on the silver coaster. "I'll get straight to the point. The mayor and I had a talk with our sister-in-law Anna this morning, and we are appalled. Apparently, she's had a hand in your and Mr. Alexander's unfortunate incidences with the press." Her voice took on a breezy, carefree quality. "I'm sure you're wondering why she targeted you like this. She wanted to tell you herself, but for the good of the town and everyone involved, she's been sent away to contemplate her actions. But I consider it my responsibility to look after her. So it's up to me to explain."

Sent away? Was that code for Anna ran away or that she was forced to take the fall for something she didn't do? "I think her reason for targeting me is pretty clear. She's a reporter. She wanted to be the one to break a big story."

"A reporter?" Poppy's voice held conviction. She released a harsh laugh. "You're so generous. Actually, Anna thought she was protecting me. She found out about your search. As usual, her ego and grand imagination about what's important outpaced her common sense. She missed the point and hit you. The misunderstanding started with a letter you found that supposedly involves me." The light, breezy tone in her voice returned. "I'm here to remedy that by giving you the right information. Is it possible for you to show me what you found?"

The letter? Poppy wasn't claiming ownership, yet she supposedly was ready to give the right information? Holland almost laughed. Poppy was toying with her. But why not play along and hear the tale?

"Yes, it's very possible." Holland took her phone from her side pocket and opened her saved photos. She got up and sat by Poppy. "This is a photo of the love letter I found from L to B. That is the torn fabric with lace that was in the letter. And this is a wedding day photo of women in your other sister-in-law's bridal party, wearing the same color dresses as the fabric."

"Oh, look at that," Poppy laughed. Underneath her practiced smile was a glimmer of something genuine. "We were all so young. Genevieve, Loretta, Callie, Tallulah, Francis…and me. I hardly recognize myself with all that dark hair. Six months later, I became a blonde. It was the best switch I ever made… along with my name."

"Beryl to Poppy?"

"Yes. Wait…who's that?" Poppy peered closer at the photo. "I've seen this picture over a dozen times. How did I miss seeing her?"

"Miss who?"

Poppy pointed to the picture on the screen. "The girl standing in the window."

Holland looked closer. All this time, she'd been focused on the women in the bridal party and hadn't noticed the dark-haired girl standing outside looking in.

"Beauty," Poppy sighed.

It took a moment to register. "That's the name of the girl in the window?" And was she also the B in the letter?

"Believe it or not, that's her real name," Poppy said wryly. She took a sip of lemonade.

What was that cautionary saying about not throwing stones? Poppy definitely couldn't throw stones or shade Beauty's way when it came to her real name. "So if Beauty wasn't part of the bridal party, who was she to the group?"

"A nuisance." Disdain grew on Poppy's face. "Her mother was a good friend of Gerard's and Genevieve's mother. Beauty was sent here to stay with them that summer. As you can see from the letter you found, she was very busy."

"So you're saying she's the B in the letter? Not you."

Poppy put her lemonade on the table, then looked Holland straight in the eye. "No. I am not." No breeziness was in her voice.

That was Poppy's tell. When she lied or was uncomfortable, light and breezy was her fallback.

Holland took a leap. "Do you know who L was?"

"I do."

"Did she run away with L?"

As Poppy studied Holland, a ghost of a smile came over her lips. "That's not my story to tell. I will say, Beauty was a foolish, selfish girl who didn't care who she hurt with her actions."

Gerard came in. Even dressed casually to match Poppy, he was every inch the dignified mayor. "Ladies, I hate to break things up, but Holland's driver is concerned about getting you to the airport on time."

The airport. Totally absorbed in getting to the bottom of the story of Beauty and L, she'd lost track of time.

Holland stood and put her phone back in her pocket. "I'd better go. Thank you for clarifying who B was. Beauty, L and the unlucky fiancé. It sounds like the name of a movie."

Sitting next to his wife, color rose into the mayor's cheeks. "Uh—yes. One with an unhappy ending., I suppose."

"For Beauty, maybe." Poppy reached over and gave Gerard's hand a squeeze. "But not for everyone."

As the Ashfords looked at each other, honest love and affection bloomed on their faces.

"Poppy and the mayor are devoted to each other. Period. And they'll do anything to protect one another. They could care less about the consequences. Also, what she knows, he knows and vice versa..."

What Charlotte had said about the Ashfords reverberated in Holland's mind.

Along with something Poppy had said a few minutes ago.

But I consider it my responsibility to look after her... That was a total lie. Poppy wasn't protecting Anna. She was protecting the person she was devoted to protecting. Gerard—Beauty's unlucky fiancé.

Holland's gaze connected with Poppy's. The woman looked uncertain.

The older woman rose from the sofa. "How rude of me. Holland, let me see you out."

As they walked down the carpeted hallway, Poppy briefly glanced at Holland. "It was an arranged engagement through their parents. The plan was to announce it during the winter holidays, to not compete with Genevieve's wedding. Aside from Gerard, Beauty and their parents, no one knew about the engagement. And only Gerard, Beauty, L and I know why the engagement ended."

"Well, I'd say he got the right woman."

"He did." Poppy said it with certainty. "Will you put the letter in your documentary?"

That morning, Holland had weighed all sides involved, like Myles had suggested. Especially the pain that exposing the affair might cause. She'd made up her mind not to reveal the contents of the letter or what she'd learned to anyone else. She had a conscience. She also had a heart that felt for other people. And her heart was now broken because she'd lost Myles.

Holland took in a breath that couldn't fill the hollowness in her chest.

But she'd done the right thing by not begging him to forgive her for ruining his life. Because no matter how hard she tried to see a way out of this, she knew it wouldn't be fair to ask him to wait until her mess, the drama that had somehow become hers, came to an end. He deserved more than that. But still, the reality of letting this amazing man go was nearly impossible to bear.

She sighed. Now was not the time to wallow in what could have been. Chasing away the image of Myles from her mind, she focused on the mayor's wife.

Beryl Franelope also had a heart buried under her force-to-be-reckoned-with exterior—and a really awful name.

Holland faced Poppy. "That's not my story to tell."

Chapter Twenty-Three

Lights twinkled below as the plane descended to the runway at LAX.

On the ground, as the pilot waited for their turn to taxi to the private terminal, Holland checked her phone for messages from Myles. There were none. But what did she expect?

Nash peered at his phone. "My agent sent a text. There's a car waiting to take us to a meeting at Burke's office."

Holland reviewed a similar message from her manager.

Nash sighed. "I'll call her and see what's up."

"Don't." The snap in Holland's voice made him look at her in shock. Right then, she was processing so much—Poppy and the mayor's confession, how a part of her wished the letter had never been found or that she'd traveled to Maryland to research the documentary in the first place.

But if she hadn't gone to Bolan, she never would have met Myles. And as much hurt and disappointment as she felt over losing him, she didn't regret what they'd shared during the few short weeks they'd been together. She'd gotten a glimpse of what true love felt like. What it was like to really matter to someone. But her relationship with Myles sadly wasn't meant to be.

If she tried to explain, Nash wouldn't understand. He only saw his own problems right now with the Gina issue. That's why he'd agreed to show up in Maryland at the worst possible time.

Barely controlling her frustration, she answered, "Whatever the reason is, let's just wait until we get there for the whole story."

"Yeah, you're right. It's probably bad news, otherwise, she would have just told me why we're meeting with everyone." Nash's expression turned grim as he rested his phone on his leg. "I'm definitely not in the rush to hear about how my career might be on the verge of taking a nosedive."

Sometime later, at an office building Burke owned outside LA, a dark-haired assistant escorted them to a white-walled conference room with beachscape paintings hanging on the wall.

Burke sat at the far end of the rectangular wood table. "Good timing. We just sat down. I think we all know each other." He pointed to a conference phone in the middle of the table. "Gina's and Nash's publicity people are on the line, along with Connie."

A man said hello and identified himself as part of Gina's publicity team. Connie's greeting also echoed through the speaker, along with another woman's.

Holland took a seat in the blue padded chair on the end of the table, opposite Burke. She did recognize the two dark-haired talent agents, Moira and Nicole. The blonde next to Burke with a no-nonsense expression was a member of his legal team.

As Nash sat next to his agent, he asked, "Where's Gina?"

Nicole, a middle-aged woman with a gray streak in her hair, barely spared him a glance. "She's in Aurora, confessing to her fiancé about what happened between the two of you, against my and her publicist's advice. We'll have to factor that situation into what we're discussing here."

Not in the mood to guess the highlights of the meeting, Holland went straight to the point. "Can someone please explain what the latest fiasco is? I'm assuming it's not just what happened in Maryland and New Jersey."

All eyes looked to Burke.

As if he'd expected it, Burke dived right in. "We have another issue surrounding the security guard who took the photo. He and the girlfriend neglected to mention he'd shown it to his girlfriend's sister. When the girlfriend discovered he was cheating on her with the sister, she came to us with information.

Her sister had a copy of the photo and recently approached a tabloid with it."

"Wait," Nash interjected. "But you told us your cybersecurity team was thorough. They said the guy hadn't shared or sent the photo anywhere."

"My team *was* thorough." Burke's tone remained calm, but his ice-blue gaze was trained on Nash. "The sister took a picture of the photo. According to the girlfriend, she didn't know about it until now. We're not sure about the guard."

"Let's sue his ass!" Nash asserted angrily. "He's broken the NDA again."

The attorney shook her head. "It's not that simple. We agreed not to enforce the original NDA in exchange for the guard and his girlfriend signing another agreement that included giving us access to their devices and permission to delete what we deemed necessary in relation to the photo."

"Maybe we're in a better position than we think," Moira said. "It's a photo of a photo. In the original one you couldn't tell it was Gina, and the quality of this one is probably worse."

"That's why we need to stay the course." Nicole leaned in and looked to everyone at the table. "If we double down on the claim that the photo is of Holland and Nash, there's a strong chance the tabloids will back off."

Gina's publicist chimed in, "That matches up with what we're planning, but with a softer touch. We've drafted a few social media posts about how it's hard to live in the public eye and face misinformation."

"But what about her fiancé and their families?" Moira asked. "What if they speak out about it?"

"We convinced Gina to just tell her fiancé and not their families…"

Pretending and playing games with the truth…

As what Myles had said played through her mind, for the first time, Holland really saw what was going on at the table.

This wasn't productive to anyone. For every truth that was upended, for every pretense that was made, someone paid a price. And for what? To save an image or a career?

It wasn't worth it. Not for her or anyone sitting at the table. Because, like Chloe had said weeks ago, both would eventually fade, but true love wouldn't. That's what was real. She didn't understand it back then, because no one had been more valuable to her than her work…until Myles.

If she could turn the clock back, she would choose him over saving Nash, the company and even the movie. But how could she have chosen Myles when she'd forgotten how to choose herself? It had been that way since directing *Shadow Valley*.

And it stopped *now*.

She raised her voice. "We're not doubling down on any claims about the photo."

Nicole looked at Holland as if that was a ridiculous thing to say. "Do you have a better solution?"

"Yes. Put the focus and money where it belongs— the movie. It's good now, and it will be great once the edits are done in postproduction. That's what I stand behind. Not the deceptions we have perpetuated and are still trying to spin now at this table. Will there be consequences? Yes. But they're a lot less costly than when you deal in the truth."

Visions of Myles played through her mind. Meeting him. Being with him. Loving him. Hurting him in the end. The last struck Holland with sorrow. "Trust me. I know."

Holland waited for Burke to try and persuade her otherwise.

She wasn't changing her mind. If their business partnership was at an end, so be it. She'd already given up enough for A & L Productions. She'd start her own company without him.

Their gazes met. Burke didn't look all that surprised.

During the long silence, he studied her face.

A flicker of understanding, maybe compassion, came and went from his eyes.

As he sat back in the chair, his gaze shifted to everyone else at the table. "You heard what my business partner said. We're changing directions. What's the plan?"

Chapter Twenty-Four

Myles walked down the path of the cemetery out-side of Philadelphia, carrying a bouquet of red roses interspersed with purple flowers. They'd been Syd-ney's favorites.

For some reason, he'd just felt he'd needed to visit her today.

From an all-knowing place, Sydney would have had a bird's-eye view of his last two weeks since leaving Bolan. It had been somewhere between what felt like a shit storm and an odd dream.

Nash Moreland had made a public statement ac-knowledging that he'd misspoken about his and Holland's relationship status. They were neither en-gaged nor on the verge of becoming engaged. Hol-land hadn't cheated on him. She'd just tried to spare him the embarrassment of his hasty words.

That revelation hadn't saved the Odom Construction contract opportunity, but according to Dante, what happened to Myles had sparked another important debate about unwarranted attacks on social media and the harm they could cause.

Myles had also finished the house. Tristan, Mace, Scott and Bastian had all pitched in to help him get it done. They'd celebrated at the local spot, and he'd felt a strange sense of belonging. That if he had a reason to be there in Bolan, it would easily feel like home.

But one important piece was missing.

Holland. Just thinking about her made him ache. So many nights, since they'd broken up, he'd closed his eyes and seen her face. When he remembered her laughter, it was as if he could feel it lingering deep in his chest.

While in Bolan he'd also learned of how the mayor's sister-in-law had been behind the release of a photo of him and Holland, and the subsequent public opinion swarming them.

If that hadn't happened, would he and Holland have made a try for a long-distance relationship? Could they have gotten past the whole Nash situation? A part of him wondered that.

But he'd never know. He'd given up on the relationship in a critical moment instead of standing by her and trying to find a way to work things out. Why would Holland want to be with him after all that?

Myles veered onto a path at the cemetery, and a tall man walked toward him. As Myles got closer to where Sydney was buried, the man with a suntanned face and salt-and-pepper hair turned toward the same area he was going.

Was the man visiting a loved one nearby? What was the etiquette for a situation like this? Did you acknowledge them or just share the silence?

Myles veered right.

The man did, too, and then he stopped where Sydney was buried.

Myles came to a halt a couple of yards away. He didn't recognize him as part of Sydney's family or friends. But the way the man's shoulders dropped and curved in as he bowed his head signaled the obvious. He'd cared deeply for her.

Jake...

Turning back the way he'd come, Myles started walking away. The right thing to do was to let Jake have his moment with Sydney.

"Are you Myles?" the man called out.

As awkward as it felt, he couldn't just ignore the guy. "Yes." Myles faced him. "Are you Jake?"

Jake nodded.

"I'll give you a minute—"

"No. It's okay. I'm on my way to the airport. I just stopped to... I just..." Jake released on long breath. "I just miss her."

Myles joined him. "I do, too."

A long beat of shared silence passed between them. He was older than Myles expected.

After retrieving Sydney's computer and phone that day from her parents' house, he'd almost looked through her photos. But the moments Jake and Sydney shared weren't his or anyone else's to see. That part of her life was private. After the estate was settled, he'd deleted everything from her devices and recycled them.

Seeing the man now, Myles could easily picture Jake and Sydney together. Knowing she'd found someone who'd made her happy raised a sense of peace in him.

Jake's grief was palpable.

Not sure if it would help, Myles took a chance and said, "Sydney really cared about you. I know you were on her mind a lot that weekend."

"I was?" A harsh chuckle shot out of Jake. "Maybe I shouldn't have been. During our last conversation, I was impatient with her. I wanted her to change her mind about the holidays. I wanted her to spend it with me...to introduce her to my kids. Sydney said she'd think about it. I keep wondering if that conversation distracted her, and that's why she fell. That if I hadn't—"

Jake's sharp intake of breath grew ragged. Tears fell from his eyes.

Myles laid a hand on Jake's shoulder for a moment. "You can't put that burden on yourself. She had a lot of distractions. The bridal shower. Preparing for her sister's wedding. How to tell her family we were splitting up. Her job. Or she could have just been really happy about moving on in her life with you. We'll never know what she was thinking. All we know for sure about that moment is that a terrible accident happened."

"Yeah… I guess you're right." As Jake released a breath, he swiped his hand down his face.

A breeze blew over them during a long beat of silence.

"What about you?" Jake asked. "How are you doing?"

"I'm good. I used to have more bad days than good days at first, but things even out."

"Have you found someone? I know that probably sounds like an odd question from me, but I know Sydney was concerned about that." He smiled sadly. "She was considering ambushing you at unexpected times with introductions to single women. Or thinking of a way to make you slow down and notice your surroundings and maybe find someone special." Jake laughed. "Anything that would encourage you to get back out there again. Her words, not mine."

Myles chuckled. "That sounds like her."

"So have you?"

A vision of Holland staring up at him with a soft smile on her face came into Myles's mind. Along with kissing her, holding her close and feeling that smile blossom under his lips. He'd never experience that again.

Reality washed over the memory like water, leaving the blank space of loss.

Myles considered the short answer. *No.* But Jake was a stranger. Why not be honest? He'd never see him again. "I did find someone…but we had too much to work through. I thought we could but she's a movie director based in LA. I'm here. Our lifestyles are different, not to mention the physical distance between us. It was a lot for us to overcome."

Jake nodded. "Sydney and I had our differences, too. I'd already raised a family. She hadn't yet. The long-distance thing. And her taste in music in the mornings."

"The saddest, slowest, lost-my-dog, lost-my-truck country music. Same songs over and over. All. The. Time."

"Exactly." Jake laughed. "I thought it was just me imagining the songs were the same. One or two of them, I'm okay. But by song twelve? I was out. And she would be so happy dancing and singing along with her curling-iron microphone in the bathroom. My dog and I would have to go for long walks just to escape."

Myles laughed with him. "Noise-canceling earbuds were my closest friends."

As they stared at Sydney's headstone, they both continued to chuckle. Suddenly, the air around them seemed lighter. The day less cloudy. Much of the sadness had dissipated.

"Well… I better get to the airport," Jake said.

"Do you need a ride?"

"No, I drove." The man extended his hand to Myles. "Thank you."

Myles returned the firm handshake. *You're wel-*

come didn't seem appropriate. "I'm glad we finally got a chance to meet."

Jake headed across the grass. After a few steps, he paused and turned to Myles. "The movie director—if you think there's a chance you could work it out with her, do it. You'll never know what's after try if you don't take the chance." He kept walking.

Hearing Sydney's words coming from Jake raised the hairs on Myles's nape. He almost asked the man to repeat himself in case he'd misheard him. But if he had, for some strange reason, Myles didn't want to know.

Meeting Jake now, he realized that the steps he and Sydney had taken to end their marriage amicably weren't made in vain. Their *try* had given Sydney and Jake weeks of happiness they might not have had.

And the choice he'd made to be with Holland had given him weeks of happiness he wouldn't trade for anything, even with all he'd faced.

It probably wasn't strange or unusual for Jake to have mentioned what he'd said to him a moment ago. Sydney had probably said it to Jake, just like she'd said it to him, thousands of times, and Jake just remembered it.

But maybe it was a sign. And maybe he now understood why Sydney had bought him the house.

"Or thinking of a way to make you slow down and notice your surroundings and maybe find someone special."

As Myles laid down the flowers, it was as if the breeze were giving him a gentle, loving push, nudging him on his way. Urging him to try.

Chapter Twenty-Five

Holland got out of the blue two-door rental she'd parked in front of Myles's house.

The For Sale sign swayed slightly in the wind on the post staked in the front yard. The two-story white clapboard home was a total change from what it had been weeks ago. Myles had decided on the dove-gray shutters and trim. The subtlety of the hues brought out the sumptuous green of the lawn and the bushes lining the red-bricked walkway.

Holland grabbed her phone from the center console, along with the key to the front door, and got out.

Peggy's assistant at Blue Sky Realty had given the key to her that morning, no questions asked about when she'd planned to return it. The young woman had only mentioned she should drop the key in the mail slot beside the office door if no one was there when she was done with it. In LA, no one would dare take such a risk.

It's intimidating and welcoming at the same time.

Myles's words on the deck of Pasture Lane Restaurant, the night they'd been formally introduced, teased a smile out of Holland.

The memory of that day made her happy and sad at the same time.

But he'd been right in what he said. Peggy's assistant's readiness to trust her had felt welcoming. Almost as if she'd come home, but still one thing was missing that would have made returning to Maryland just right.

Sadness pinged in the emptiness that grown wider inside Holland since she and Myles had broken up. Was the idea of putting a bid on the house a bad one? It had come to her last night on the red-eye from LA. She needed a home base while she worked on developing her film project.

She was going ahead with the wine cellar house… and the mural house. She'd received an envelope in the mail from Charlotte with a phone number and an address for where it was located two towns over from Bolan. The boutique owner wouldn't say where she got it, but Holland suspected it was Poppy. A thank-you for not exposing the mayor? Probably not. But providing something more tempting to focus on— that was definitely a tactic Poppy would use, and Holland was accepting it.

But she'd wanted to take one more look at the

house that had set her on a journey she'd never expected to embark on before making up her mind.

Holland pushed aside pain and the memories and
went inside.

The polished wood floors and handrail to the
staircase gleamed in the light shining through the
back sliding door. The faint smell of paint lingered
in the air along with...

No. That was pine oil. She was imagining the fragrance of Myles's woodsy cologne.

Walking farther inside the living room, Holland
was drawn to the fireplace. As she ran her hand over
the mantel, memories played through her mind of
bricks tumbling to the floor and looking up to find
Myles's sexy, scowling face. Another raised up of the
two of them finding the letter followed by a montage
of moments in the house with him. And how their
kisses had ignited sparks of desire that had burned
hotter than any flame in that fireplace ever would.

As Holland dropped her hand from the mantel, the
memories faded, but the longing for Myles remained.
But wanting him to be there with her so badly was
expected, right? Someday, she would find a way to
resolve him not being there with her to share in the
things she looked forward to like waking up to the
sound of birds, staring blissfully into a fire crackling
in the fireplace. Seeing the sun rise and set behind
the tall trees, Entertaining Chloe and Tristan, and
the other couples she'd come to know, in the dining
room or on the back deck.

She could almost hear the laughter and lively conversation. As she imagined them there, she couldn't help but see Myles helping her entertain the group. They wouldn't be relegated to the "kid's" table on date night anymore. They would be free to hold hands, smile at their own private jokes, and exchange as many long lingering glances and kisses as they wanted.

But since Myles would be there, it would have be with some other guy. She couldn't imagine that, yet. And from the ache in her heart, she doubted that day would ever come. Or at least not for a long while. It would be hard to top someone like Myles.

Would he find someone? As much as it hurt to think about that, she hoped he would. Someone who would make him laugh and smile often. Help him fix things around the house. Bring him coffee in bed. Join him for long luxurious showers.

A vision of her doing those things came into her mind and she cleared it away. Bottom line, she just wished Myles happiness and all he wanted from the world. He deserved it.

Mind made up, Holland slipped her phone from her pocket and dialed the real estate office.

Peggy answered on the second ring. "Blue Sky Realty."

"Hello, it's Holland Ainsley. I picked up the key for Myles's house—I mean, the one on Oakview Road—this morning."

"Yes. I'm so glad you called."

"I want to buy the house." The words tumbled out of Holland's mouth.

But saying it felt right. She couldn't imagine working on the development of her dream documentary anywhere else.

"Oh dear…there's a problem with that. My assistant didn't know. That house is already off the market."

Disappointment sliced through Holland's excitement. "Who bought it?" She shouldn't have asked. Of course, Peggy wouldn't tell her that information.

Movement from the door behind Holland caught her attention, and a familiar voice drifted over her. "No one bought it. Because it's not for sale anymore."

Startled, Holland turned around.

Myles walked farther inside the house, looking all kinds of wonderful, and her heart slammed against her rib cage, then shifted to an uneven pitter-patter.

As he stood in front of her, his gaze briefly dropped to her phone, reminding her that Peggy was still on the line. But surprise stole her words.

Sensing her plight, he gently slipped the phone from her grasp. "Hi. It's Myles… It's okay. I understand. Sometimes things get lost in communication." His gaze met Holland's. "Yes…yes, I'll explain everything to her. Thank you. Goodbye."

Myles tapped the screen, ending the call. "Peggy said to tell you that she's sorry for the confusion. But it's not her fault, it's mine."

"Oh?" As she accepted her phone from him, the warmth from his fingers briefly seeped into hers.

"Yeah. I should explain." A small smile tipped up his mouth, but as he glanced down, a moment of uncertainty shadowed his eyes. "I called Peggy at her house early this morning and told her the place was off the market. I'm keeping it."

"You are? I mean, you should, especially after all the work you put into it. It's beautiful."

"Yes, very beautiful." His gaze lingered on her face, reminding her of how he'd looked at her in the past.

Or she was only imagining he was looking at her that way. Why would he do that now?

Afraid her eyes would mirror the longing and regret practically spilling out of her, Holland glanced down and stuck her phone in her back pocket.

Curiosity made her ask, "What changed your mind?"

"The work you and I put into this house. Strangers don't belong in here."

Something in his voice sparked hope and her gaze flew to his face. The same longing she felt was in his eyes.

Myles took her hand in his. "We do."

Was he saying what she thought he was? Caught in a swirl of hope and disbelief, Holland wasn't sure what to say. "You mean us…here…together?"

"Yes. That's what I want." He tugged her closer into his sphere of warmth. Hopefulness and something she was afraid to name was in his eyes. "I want us to share sunrises and sunsets, cold nights in front of this fireplace. I want to share coffee with you in the morning and hear how you plan to conquer the world with your films. I want to see you off at the airport and be there to pick you up when you get back."

That all sounded wonderful and her heart wanted to dive into that future, but... "You said you didn't see yourself in my world."

"I don't." He tightened his hold a little, as if afraid she'd pull away. "Hollywood will never be my style. But it's part of you. And New York could never completely be your style, either. But it's part of me. But those differences don't have to mean the end of us." He glanced around the house. "This could be our home. Sure, we'll have to leave to oversee projects, but this could be the place we always return to...if that's something you wanted to try out with me. But if you don't want—"

Holland cupped his face and pressed her lips to his. She *did* want, with every fiber of her being.

Myles kissed her back, exploring the curves and hollows of her mouth so deliciously that she rose on her toes for more.

A long moment later, they broke apart. As she took in a much-needed breath, she leaned into him, absorbing his warmth, his presence. She reveled in happiness.

He smiled down at her. "Just to be clear, that's a yes?"

"You know it is. I love you." Being able to say those words felt so right.

"I love you. too." As he stroked his finger down

her cheek, his smile sobered a little. "And just to be clear, I know we'll have to weather some storms because of our careers or just life in general, but I won't back away from them."

"Neither will I. Whatever it is, we'll find a way through it."

Those promises felt like solemn vows. Solid and real.

"Where do we start?" As she slid her arms up his chest and wrapped them loosely around his neck he grasped her waist.

He gave her one of those small sexy smiles that always weakened her knees. "I was thinking we should seal our deal upstairs."

"I'm all for doing that. But a bed would be a lot nicer place to have a reunion than on the floor."

"I agree." He punctuated his reply with a lingering kiss. "And that's why there's a bed already there with those fluffy pillows you like. And later on, when you get hungry, there's food and champagne, courtesy of Chefs Philippa and Dominic in the refrigerator."

Of course, Myles had made a plan. Holland loved that about him, but she couldn't resist teasing him. "Wait a minute. Peggy's assistant had all three keys and gave me one of them. How did you get in here?"

He flashed a slightly mischievous smile. "The side door to the garage. I didn't get around to repairing the lock."

"Oh—so you broke in."

"I can't break into my own house."

"I don't know. It still kind of sounds like trespassing."

"That's stretching the definition a lot. But in some ways, I'm a fan of trespassing." He leaned in, aiming for a kiss. "It brought me you."

* * * * *

COMING NEXT MONTH FROM

⊕HARLEQUIN®
SPECIAL EDITION™

#2971 FORTUNE'S FATHERHOOD DARE
The Fortunes of Texas: Hitting the Jackpot • by Makenna Lee

When bartender Damon Fortune Maloney boasts that he can handle any kid, single mom Sari Keeling dares him to watch her two rambunctious boys for just one day. It's game on, but Damon soon discovers that parenthood is tougher than he thought—and so is resisting Sari.

#2972 HER MAN OF HONOR
Love, Unveiled • by Teri Wilson

Bridal-advice columnist and jilted bride Everly England couldn't have predicted the feelings a sympathetic kiss from her best friend would ignite in her. Henry Aston knows the glamorous city girl is terrified romance will ruin their friendship. But this stand-in groom plans to win her "I do" after all!

#2973 MEETING HIS SECRET DAUGHTER
Forever, Texas • by Marie Ferrarella

When nurse Riley Robertson brought engineer Matt O'Brien to Forever to meet the daughter he never knew he had, she was only planning to help Matt see that he can be the father his little girl needs. But could the charming new dad be the man Riley didn't know she needed? And are the three ready to become a forever family?

#2974 THE RANCHER'S BABY
Aspen Creek Bachelors • by Kathy Douglass

Suddenly named guardian of a baby girl, rancher Isaac Montgomery gamely steps up for daddy duty, with the help of new neighbor Savannah Rogers. Sparks fly, but Savannah's reserved even as their feelings heat up. Are Isaac and his baby too painful a reminder of her heartbreaking loss? Or do they hold the key to healing?

#2975 ALL'S FAIR IN LOVE AND WINE
Love in the Valley • by Michele Dunaway

Unexpectedly back in town, Jack Clayton is acting as if he never crushed Sierra James's teenage heart. When he offers to buy her family's vineyard, the former navy lieutenant knows Jack is turning on the charm, but no way is she planning to melt for him again. But will denying what she still feels for Jack prove to be a victory she can savor?

#2976 NO RINGS ATTACHED
Once Upon a Wedding • by Mona Shroff

Fleeing her own nuptials wasn't part of wedding planner Sangeeta Parikh's plan. Neither was stumbling into chef Sonny Pandya's arms and becoming an internet sensation! So why not fake a relationship so Sangeeta can save face and her job, and to get Sonny much-needed exposure for his restaurant? It's a good plan for two commitmentphobes...until their fake commitment starts to feel all too real.

Get 4 FREE REWARDS!

We'll send you 2 FREE Books <u>plus</u> 2 FREE Mystery Gifts.

FREE Value Over **$20**

Both the **Harlequin® Special Edition** and **Harlequin® Heartwarming™** series feature compelling novels filled with stories of love and strength where the bonds of friendship, family and community unite.

YES! Please send me 2 FREE novels from the Harlequin Special Edition or Harlequin Heartwarming series and my 2 FREE gifts (gifts are worth about $10 retail). After receiving them, if I don't wish to receive any more books, I can return the shipping statement marked "cancel." If I don't cancel, I will receive 6 brand-new Harlequin Special Edition books every month and be billed just $5.49 each in the U.S. or $6.24 each in Canada, a savings of at least 12% off the cover price, or 4 brand-new Harlequin Heartwarming Larger-Print books every month and be billed just $6.24 each in the U.S. or $6.74 each in Canada, a savings of at least 19% off the cover price. It's quite a bargain! Shipping and handling is just 50¢ per book in the U.S. and $1.25 per book in Canada.* I understand that accepting the 2 free books and gifts places me under no obligation to buy anything. I can always return a shipment and cancel at any time by calling the number below. The free books and gifts are mine to keep no matter what I decide.

Choose one: ☐ **Harlequin Special Edition**
(235/335 HDN GRJV)

☐ **Harlequin Heartwarming**
Larger-Print
(161/361 HDN GRJV)

Name (please print)

Address   Apt. #

City   State/Province   Zip/Postal Code

Email: Please check this box ☐ if you would like to receive newsletters and promotional emails from Harlequin Enterprises ULC and its affiliates. You can unsubscribe anytime.

Mail to the **Harlequin Reader Service:**
IN U.S.A.: P.O. Box 1341, Buffalo, NY 14240-8531
IN CANADA: P.O. Box 603, Fort Erie, Ontario L2A 5X3

Want to try 2 free books from another series! Call 1-800-873-8635 or visit www.ReaderService.com.

---

*Terms and prices subject to change without notice. Prices do not include sales taxes, which will be charged (if applicable) based on your state or country of residence. Canadian residents will be charged applicable taxes. Offer not valid in Quebec. This offer is limited to one order per household. Books received may not be as shown. Not valid for current subscribers to the Harlequin Special Edition or Harlequin Heartwarming series. All orders subject to approval. Credit or debit balances in a customer's account(s) may be offset by any other outstanding balance owed by or to the customer. Please allow 4 to 6 weeks for delivery. Offer available while quantities last.

Your Privacy—Your information is being collected by Harlequin Enterprises ULC, operating as Harlequin Reader Service. For a complete summary of the information we collect, how we use this information and to whom it is disclosed, please visit our privacy notice located at corporate.harlequin.com/privacy-notice. From time to time we may also exchange your personal information with reputable third parties. If you wish to opt out of this sharing of your personal information, please visit readerservice.com/consumerschoice or call 1-800-873-8635. **Notice to California Residents**—Under California law, you have specific rights to control and access your data. For more information on these rights and how to exercise them, visit corporate.harlequin.com/california-privacy.

HSEHW22R3

HARLEQUIN
PLUS

Try the best multimedia subscription service for romance readers like you!

Read, Watch and Play.

Experience the easiest way to get the romance content you crave.

Start your **FREE TRIAL** at
<u>www.harlequinplus.com/freetrial</u>.